Guardian Angel House

A Holocaust Remembrance Book for Young Readers

Guardian Angel House

Kathy Clark

Second Story Press

Library and Archives Canada Cataloguing in Publication

Clark, Kathy, 1953-

Guardian angel house / by Kathy Clark.

(Holocaust remembrance series for young readers)

ISBN 978-1-897187-58-6

1. Holocaust, Jewish (1939-1945)—Hungary—Juvenile fiction. I. Title. II. Series: Holocaust remembrance book for young readers

PS8555.L3703G83 2009   jC813'.6   C2009-901492-0

Edited by Sarah Swartz
Cover and text design by Melissa Kaita
Printed and bound in Canada
Cover photo © Corbis

Second Story Press gratefully acknowledges the support of the Ontario Arts Council and the Canada Council for the Arts for our publishing program. We acknowledge the financial support of the Government of Canada through the Book Publishing Industry Development Program.

Mixed Sources
Product group from well-managed
forests, and other controlled sources
www.fsc.org Cert no. SW-COC-002358
© 1996 Forest Stewardship Council

Published by
Second Story Press
20 Maud Street, Suite 401
Toronto, Ontario, Canada
M5V 2M5
www.secondstorypress.ca

For my mother and my aunt — the real Vera and Susan

*And for the Sisters of Charity of the Guardian Angel Convent
who through their courageous sacrifice saved the lives of
more than one hundred Jewish children.*

Contents

Introduction

Guardian Angel House is based on a true story. There really was a convent in Budapest, Hungary, run by the Sisters of Charity of St. Vincent de Paul. Because of the protection and service that it offered to the poor people of the city, especially to children, the convent was nicknamed "Guardian Angel House."

During World War II, German Nazis invaded Hungary on March 19, 1944, and began to capture and kill the Jews of the city. In response, the nuns of the convent decided to shelter Jewish children in an attempt to save them from the Nazi brutality.

Hungary is located in Central Europe. Its capital city, Budapest, is divided by the Danube River. The western side of the city, Buda, is hilly, while the eastern side, Pest, is flat. Seven bridges cross the river to connect Buda and Pest.

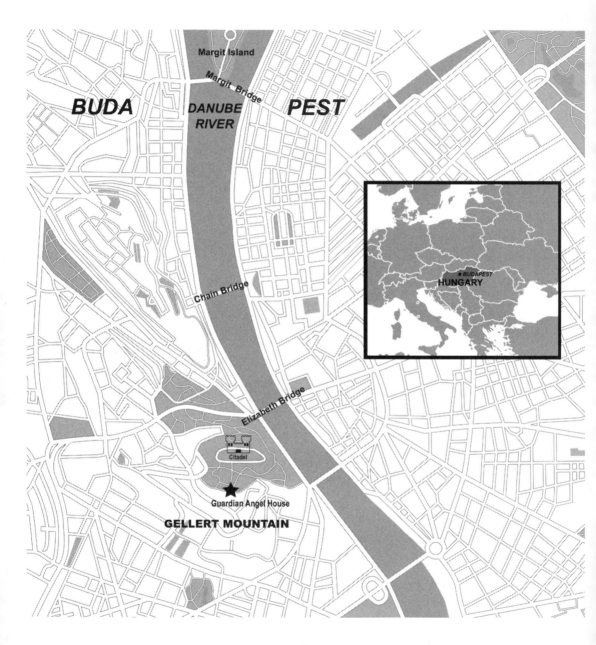

2

The convent, Guardian Angel House, is on the side of Gellert Mountain, one of Buda's large hills. On the hilltop, which is relatively flat, is an ancient citadel that provides a commanding view of the city. It is also a natural fortification against enemies – which is why the Nazis used it as one of their bases.

World War II lasted from 1939 to 1945. Throughout this time, Adolf Hitler strove to make Nazi Germany the "ruler" of the world. Germany invaded one European country after another, starting with Poland. Part of Hitler's plan was to wipe out all Jews and other minority groups who did not fit his image of "perfection". He set in motion a plan that would eliminate all Jews, Gypsies, people with disabilities, and others from Europe. He established several prisons – or concentration camps – to which he deported thousands of people from the countries his army invaded. In these camps, the people were forced to work under extremely harsh conditions. Many were killed with poisonous gas and their bodies burned. Anyone found helping these people was also put to death.

Hungary was one of the last countries to be invaded by Nazi Germany. Even though Hungary had passed several laws limiting the activities of its Jewish citizens between 1938 and 1944, it did not give in completely to Nazi pressure to destroy its Jewish population until the Nazis occupied the country. Before the occupation, Hungary, hoping to fend off the Nazis, had already limited the kind of work Jews could do, the buildings they could enter, and the places where they could shop. However, they did not force Jews to live in ghettos or wear the yellow star that Hitler used to identify them in public. Jewish men were sent to labor camps, but conditions there were not as harsh as those of the concentration camps in other countries. Many people in Hungary believed that what was happening in other countries would never happen in their country.

All this changed when Nazi Germany invaded Hungary. Between March 19, 1944, and January 17, 1945, when Hungary was liberated by the Russians, the Nazis killed 550,000 Hungarian Jews. They achieved this with cooperation from the newly empowered Nazi Arrow Cross Party of Hungary – a pro-Nazi political party that ruled Hungary from October 15, 1944, to January 1945.

But some Hungarian Jews were saved. Several individuals and institutions were willing to risk everything, even their lives, to protect or hide Jews. Among them were people such as Swedish diplomat Raoul Wallenberg and Giorgio Perlasca, from the Spanish Embassy. They used their positions of power and authority to obtain fake passports and identity papers for Jews who otherwise would have been deported to concentration camps. Some, such as the Sisters of Guardian Angel House, used their institutions to protect Jews.

This is the story of Susan and Vera, two of the one hundred and twenty Jewish girls in the care of the nuns at Guardian Angel House Convent during World War II.

Part One
The Convent

Chapter 1

Footprints

December 1943

Susan felt the rumble of marching boots long before she heard their heavy tread on the staircase. They penetrated her dream and sent a chill of dread through her body. By the time they came to a halt outside the apartment door, she was fully awake and sitting up in bed, her down blanket pulled protectively up around her neck and shoulders. She glanced at the clock. Ten minutes past nine. It was only minutes since she had climbed into the warm comfort of her bed, heard Papa's soothing voice bidding her goodnight, and felt his whiskers brush her cheek as she closed her eyes.

She held her breath during the eternal moment of silence that hung in the air before the dull pounding of fists on the front door of the apartment.

"Open up!" a rough voice yelled.

Susan dropped her blanket and slipped out of bed. Cautiously, she opened her bedroom door in time to see Papa open the front door. Susan recognized the dark olive green of the soldiers' uniforms.

One soldier shoved a letter into her father's face. "You are to report to the office on Duna Street at the break of day!"

"No need to bring any luggage," another soldier sneered. "You will be supplied with whatever you need." Then the soldiers turned on their heels and left.

Papa looked for a long time at the envelope in his hand. Methodically, he turned it over and pried open the gummed flap, extracting a single sheet of paper. When he looked up, his forehead beneath his short, curly red hair was furrowed.

"I'm being sent away to work in a labor camp," he said, walking to the table and wrapping an arm around Mama. "It won't be for too long, you'll see. At least I will have work again," he ended with strained cheerfulness. It was then that he noticed Susan standing by the bedroom door. He went over, knelt in front of her, and held her close.

"Susan, I will miss you. But I'm sure that you will all be fine. You are a big girl now, almost eleven. You must be Mama's strength now. Help her all you can," he said into the thick tangle of red curls that draped around her shoulders. Susan understood. Mama loved Papa very much. She always said that together they were strong. As long as they were together, Mama could face the increasing hardships they were subjected to every day. As long as she had Papa, she could face anything. Now Papa was leaving.

Susan squared her shoulders and straightened her back. She nodded at her father with all the confidence she could muster. In truth, she was frightened. She had so many questions. But Papa was leaving in the morning. She wanted him to know that he could count on her.

For almost as long as Susan could remember, the war had been an ominous presence in her life. Every morning at breakfast, as she sat with her steaming cup of cocoa and the fresh, warm crescent roll that Papa bought daily from the corner bakery, she listened as he read pieces aloud from the newspaper. One of her earliest memories was

Susan and Vera

of the heavy silence that enveloped the kitchen after he read about the night of November 9, 1938, when thousands of Jewish businesses across Germany were robbed and destroyed by the Nazis. *Kristallnacht,* the night of broken glass, it was called, because of all the glass from shattered Jewish shop windows that littered the streets.

Mama's face had gone deathly white and her lips trembled. "What will happen to us?" she whispered.

"That could never happen here in Hungary," Papa had reassured her.

"That could never happen in Hungary," became Papa's refrain throughout the years as he read of the ever-increasing hardships faced by Jews across Europe. Though their lives as Jews living in the capital city of Budapest had become more difficult, things were never as bad as what was taking place in other countries that were invaded by Germany. There, Susan knew, most Jews had lost their homes and were forced to live in ghettos. They were forced to wear a yellow star on their clothing and were restricted from participating in many normal activities. So far, Germany had left Hungary alone. The Hungarian prime minister had managed to resist much of the Nazi pressure to subjugate the Jewish citizens of Hungary.

Even after Papa lost his job at the university, he managed to maintain a positive outlook.

But now it was beginning to happen to them as well. There had been rumors of men summoned in the night, sent by truckloads to distant labor camps, where they worked long hours in quarries, weapons factories, and mines. Susan had overheard many whispered conversations about the harsh conditions that exhausted the men both physically and emotionally.

Before, it had always been other people who were taken away. Now it was her father. But Papa was strong. *Stronger than most*, she thought proudly. He had always been athletic and fit. A professor of history and literature at the university, he also coached the men's soccer team.

"I have to show those boys that I, too, can do everything I demand from them," he would remind Mama when she worried that he was overexerting himself. Even after he was dismissed because he was Jewish – Jews were no longer allowed to teach in educational institutions – he exercised daily, often running over the bridge and around the entire circumference of Margit Island. *Those labor camps won't hurt him*, Susan reassured herself.

Susan and Vera's parents

"I will take care of Mama," she promised her father. "And I'll help her take care of Vera and Tomas too. But you will be back soon, right?" She had to add that last half-pleading sentence. This time Papa failed to respond with his usual optimism. Instead, he straightened up, rumpled her hair, and told her that it was time to return to bed. He and Mama had a lot to talk about in their few remaining hours.

As she obediently turned to go, he followed her to her room. Gently, he woke little Vera and explained to her that he would have to go away for a while and would be leaving very early in the morning. Vera, still half asleep, mumbled something, and Susan saw her slender white arms briefly encircle Papa's neck before she snuggled back into her covers. Papa knelt by the bed for a long while, looking down at Vera's sleeping form till Susan thought that perhaps he, too, had fallen asleep. At last he stood, wiped his eyes, and came to her bed. There was no need for him to say anything more. Susan hugged her father for a long time, willing her arms to remember the strength of his body, her nose to retain the sweet lingering smell of his pipe tobacco, her cheeks to feel forever the rough stubble of his short beard. She wanted to tell him again that she loved him and that he needn't worry, she would help Mama. But the big lump in her throat prevented her from uttering a sound.

Early next morning, Susan woke to the clatter of dishes coming from the kitchen. Darkness still enveloped the room that she shared with her five-year-old sister, Veronika, or Vera, as they called her. Recalling the events of the previous night, she climbed out of bed with apprehension and tiptoed to the bedroom door. She saw Mama, with two-month-old Tomas balanced on her hip, clearing away the last of the breakfast dishes.

"I'd better go now, I guess," said Papa softly. "It wouldn't do to be late." He stood and pulled Mama and Tomas into a tight embrace. Her parents stood silently, staring into each other's eyes, for so long that Susan worried that Papa would indeed be late. Would those soldiers who came last night hurt him if he didn't show up on time? She was about to rush in and tug on his jacket pocket when Papa released Mama and hurried to the door at the other end of the kitchen. Without looking back, he was gone.

Mama extinguished the single candle flickering in its clay holder on the table and, clutching Tomas, rushed to the window that overlooked the courtyard. Susan ran to her side. They hugged each other, then pressed their foreheads against the thin pane of glass, straining to catch one last glimpse of Papa.

He emerged from the stairwell below them and made his way across the open courtyard to the large doors leading into the street. They gazed in silence at the succession of faint footprints that appeared behind him in the thin sprinkling of fresh snow. For the first time, his tall, strong body seemed small as he walked alone in the dim light. Fresh flakes of snow drifted down and, within moments, erased his footprints.

Chapter 2
Aunt Isi

It was Aunt Isi who helped them get through those first few days of anxiety and adjustment to life without Papa. Aunt Isi always sensed when Mama needed her and never failed to give her support. On the day Papa left, she dropped by after work, bringing with her a rare treat, a small chicken for Mama to cook for their dinner. The comforting aroma of the roasted chicken helped to restore some sense of normalcy to their home.

"We can't ignore it any longer," Aunt Isi told Mama soberly. "The conditions for Jews are getting much worse, even here in Hungary. We have to do something to save your children." She paced the small kitchen back and forth – as was her custom when she was thinking. Mama sat in her chair, rocking baby Tomas.

"There is nothing to be done," said Mama. A tear trickled down the smooth surface of her cheek.

"There are still countries where Jews are safe and accepted, where there is no persecution of Jews. I could help you leave here."

"Never!" Mama replied at once. "We could never leave here. How would Moritz ever find us? I have no way of contacting him now. I don't even know where they are taking him. Besides, there is no safe place for a Jew. And how could we leave our home?" Mama waved an arm around their comfortable apartment.

Susan sat at the kitchen table, drawing on the fresh pad of white paper that Aunt Isi had brought for her. Listening closely, she let out a sigh of relief. She agreed with Mama. They couldn't leave their home. The spacious living room held the soft sofa and intricately carved glass bookcase that used to belong to Mama's parents. The shiny wood surfaces in every room were covered with dainty lace doilies crocheted by her grandmother. On the walls hung framed scenes of country roads and quaint villages that Mama had painted over the years. From the open bedroom door drifted the sound of Vera's animated voice as she played with her doll collection. All their family's memories were here.

Aunt Isi stopped pacing, suddenly looking weary. She sat down next to Susan.

"I guess I should start peeling the potatoes," she said, her voice resigned. She reached into the basket beside Mama and pulled out a large brown potato.

Even though they called her "aunt," Susan knew that Isi was not a blood relative. You could tell by looking at her that she was not part of their family. Her height and fair complexion were a sharp contrast to Mama's dark hair and small frame.

Aunt Isi always wore her straight, blond hair pulled tightly back into a fancy knot at the nape of her neck, with never a single strand out of place. Though she looked stern, she was kind and gentle, and they all loved her dearly.

Susan considered herself an artist like Mama and often thought in terms of how she would draw things. *If I ever drew a picture of Aunt Isi,* mused Susan, *I would start with dark, straight lines and sharp corners. Then, when the picture was finished, I would have to smudge the edges of the lines just a bit so that they blended in softly with the background.*

Aunt Isi's real name was Isabella, but no one ever called her that. "Isi" was more suited to her practical, take-charge attitude. It was this characteristic that had drawn her and Mama together as children and formed a bond that strengthened with each passing year.

"Isi always looked out for me," Mama told Susan the day she explained to her that Aunt Isi was not really her aunt. "I was always rather naïve, I suppose, wanting to think the best of everyone. But unfortunately, some people took advantage of that. Isi always came to my rescue. She could never stand to see anyone treated unfairly. And I didn't have any sisters. Besides," she had added, "no real sister could ever be closer to me than Isi is."

Aunt Isi was Catholic, but their different religions never seemed to be an issue between her and Mama. She had been as outraged as Mama and Papa when Papa lost his job or when they were forbidden to go to the theater or enter certain buildings. The only thing about which Mama and Aunt Isi ever seemed at odds was the fact that at thirty-four years of age, Aunt Isi was still not married.

"My job with the government is too demanding. I don't have the time and energy for family life. Besides, I've got you," she said jokingly whenever Mama and Papa suggested that she meet some male friend of theirs. "You're all the family I need."

"You are just too stubborn and independent," Mama would counter, shaking her head.

Susan glanced up at Aunt Isi. She was glad that Aunt Isi was stubborn and independent. It is what gave her the courage to remain loyal to them despite the growing hatred toward the Jews of the city.

Unlike my friends, thought Susan. They had stopped playing with her just because she was Jewish. She recalled her shock and hurt the first time it happened, the day that her friend Ildiko began to ignore her. It was on the same morning that Papa had read the news out loud at breakfast about the Jews of Poland being forced to wear a yellow star whenever they went outside. Susan was younger then and didn't understand why her mother and father were so disturbed. She went down to the courtyard to play with Ildiko, as she did every morning before they left for school. Ildiko was already there, playing hopscotch. As Susan approached, Ildiko picked up a stone and threw it in the puddle next to Susan, spraying muddy water all over her.

"Hey, what did you do that for?" Susan cried out.

"What does it matter?" Ildiko retorted, "My father says you're a filthy Jew anyway. And I'm not allowed to play with you anymore." Then she turned and ran into the building.

Susan stood rooted to the spot, confused. Why did Ildiko say that? She had been perfectly clean until Ildiko sprayed the dirty water on her. Slowly, she went back upstairs. Mama wiped her coat off with angry dabs as Susan told her what had happened. Watching her, Susan had another thought.

"Mama, are we bad because we are Jewish?"

"No, dear, of course not," Mama said. She hugged Susan close to her. "Ildiko and her father don't understand what they are saying. They've been caught up in this wave of hatred that is spreading across the country. They have forgotten the good times our families have shared in the past. Jewish people are both good and bad – just like other people."

Mama's words were comforting at the time. But they didn't help Susan as gradually most of her old friends refused to play with her. They turned their backs when she approached and pretended not to hear when she spoke.

Thank goodness, Aunt Isi was not that kind of a friend. Instead, Aunt Isi worried about Susan's family.

Chapter 3

The Decision

February 1944

"Don't be silly, Isi!" Mama retorted the first time Aunt Isabella made the suggestion that at least the girls should be sent into hiding. "There is no safe place for a Jew anywhere."

"Rose, you must listen. Things are getting worse. The Germans are increasing the pressure on us to put Jews in a ghetto or deport them. I have heard rumors that if we don't comply, Hungary, too, will be invaded by the Nazis. You must think of your children, Rose. Many people are going into hiding. You know what is happening in Poland, Holland, and Denmark since the Nazis' invasion."

Mama interrupted, "But Moritz always said that can never happen here. It will never get that bad. Not in Hungary."

"But now Moritz is gone because of the pressure exerted by the

Nazis," continued Aunt Isi. "Besides, this place I'm talking about, the convent, is different. It's just over on the Buda side of the city, on Gellert Mountain. The Mother Superior there and the nuns in her charge firmly believe that all people are equal. They know that the Nazi influence on our country is wrong, and they have offered help to those who need it. There are several Jewish girls there already, living with the novices and nuns." Aunt Isabella stopped her pacing to catch her breath.

"And even if they weren't willing to protect Jews," she continued in a more even tone, "even if the girls had to hide who they truly are, it would be all right. Look," she said, pulling out from her skirt pocket a large brown envelope folded in half. "You remember my cousin Paul who lives in Eszterhaz? He has two daughters who are the same ages as Vera and Susan. They are planning to leave the country soon. He made copies of his daughters' birth and baptismal certificates and gave me the originals. Vera and Susan can use them and pass as Catholics. The nuns have always operated an orphanage for girls. People are used to seeing young girls there. They have even nicknamed the convent 'Guardian Angel House'."

"No!" Mama broke in firmly. "My girls will never pretend to be Catholics. We will not hide who we are. We are proud to be Jews. We don't need Catholic charity."

Aunt Isabella dropped the envelope onto Mama's lap. She walked to the window. She reached out and angrily plucked a petal off the solitary red rose that Mama kept there in a slender glass vase.

With her back to Mama, she said quietly, "You are being unkind, Rose. Haven't we always been best friends? We never labeled each other Jew or Catholic. It pains me to see your suffering so because of this insanity that has possessed Europe. And I'm not the only Catholic who feels this way." Aunt Isabella turned back to face Mama. "There are many others and not just Catholics. There are people of all races and religions who recognize the horror of what is happening. How can we put a stop to this if you don't allow us to help?"

Aunt Isabella walked over to Mama and stooped down in front of her. "Please, Rose, trust me. Trust the others. We want to help you and your children."

Mama hid her face in her hands. "I'm sorry, Isi. I didn't mean to hurt your feelings. I know you only want what is best for us. I just don't

The Convent of the Sisters of Charity of St. Vincent de Paul would become a safe haven for Susan and Vera during the Nazi occupation of Hungary.

know who to trust anymore." Mama looked up into Aunt Isabella's eyes. "I wish Moritz were here. He always said we must be proud to be Jewish no matter what. Am I betraying him and all the other Jews who are suffering, if I pretend the girls are Catholic?"

Susan watched and listened from the corner where she sat cuddled with Vera, who was looking through a worn picture book. Susan wanted to run to Mama's side and insist that she would never leave, but something about the intensity in the women's voices held her back. She didn't know what was right anymore. Though she had turned twelve last month and felt almost grown-up, she knew that these grave decisions were hard even for her mother to make.

Three days later, the owner of the corner store refused to serve Mama. Then their neighbor told her that women, too, were being sent to labor camps. Finally, Mama gave in to Aunt Isi's pleas.

Chapter 4

Leaving Home

March 1944

"Don't worry, Mama, I will always take care of Vera." These were Susan's last words to her mother as they left. She repeated the words now, over and over in her mind, hoping to boost her courage.

On this early Sunday morning, three months after her father had been taken away, Susan clutched Aunt Isi's hand as if the pressure of her clasp could still the fluttering in the pit of her stomach. They were on their way to the convent on Gellert Mountain – two Jewish girls going to live with a group of nuns and already pretending they were part of the scattering of Catholics heading off to Sunday Mass.

She peered past her aunt at Vera whose golden curls bobbed up and down as she skipped happily along. Susan frowned. Vera wasn't the one who needed to be taken care of. Mama and baby Tomas needed her too. She had failed in keeping her promise to Papa. Would she fail in keeping her promise to Mama as well?

I will always take care of Vera, she repeated to herself, in a final attempt to regain her composure. One thing was sure. Now that they were on their way, she didn't want Aunt Isi to see her worry. Aunt Isi was doing what she thought was best for them. She was counting on Susan to act grown up.

"You are helping me by leaving," Mama had said, trying to comfort Susan. "It will make all the difference in the world to me to know that at least my girls are safe. I know it is what Papa would want as well." Susan wondered now if perhaps the tremor in her mother's voice had been uncertainty, rather than sorrow. Perhaps she should have put up more of a fuss. Then they might still be with Mama. Would their family ever be together again?

Susan glanced toward the sun that was trying to break through the mottled haze of clouds. She shivered and pulled her coat tightly around her, flinging her thick braids over her shoulders. The early March wind still held a lingering breath of winter. Maybe by summertime they would be back home. Maybe Papa would be back by then too.

They turned a corner – out of the narrow street lined with solid old apartment buildings onto the boulevard that circled the inner city of Budapest – and walked toward the Danube River just a couple of blocks away. The familiar odor of decaying fish and seaweed mixed with the fumes from rumbling diesel trucks, the clanging of the streetcar, and the sing-song cry of old Mr. Lukacs from his newsstand on the corner were comforting signs – signs of normal, everyday life. And there in front of them, just a couple of blocks away, were the massive concrete pillars marking the entrance onto Margit Bridge.

Susan smiled at the sight of the bridge that connected the two halves of the city to Margit Island in the middle of the Danube. Her fondest memories were of family picnics on the island and swimming in its various pools. She could almost smell the tantalizing aroma of fried chicken and freshly sliced cucumbers that Mama always served on their picnics. The bridge had stood there for a very long time. *I will see it again soon*, she promised herself.

She glanced through a large café window they were passing. Elegantly dressed men and women sipped their early morning espresso. At one table, a girl about Susan's age sat laughing with her parents. A mixture of longing and resentment filled Susan. The muscles in her throat tightened and she found it difficult to swallow. She, too, ought

Margit Bridge connected Buda and Pest. Susan's family picnicked on Margit Island in the middle of the Danube River.

to be able to sit there with her parents. But because she was Jewish, she and her family were different. They weren't even allowed into the café any more. It wasn't fair!

More than anything, Susan wanted to be like everybody else. Now she was going to a place, a convent, where she would be even more different than she had been before.

She felt the earth beneath her feet rumble before she saw the bright yellow of the approaching streetcar round the bend. This rumble, which before had always filled her with excited anticipation, now filled her with dread.

"There's our streetcar. Let's hurry, girls," said Aunt Isi, pulling them along. "We still have a long way to go and we don't want to be late." The three of them picked up their pace. Breathless, they arrived beside the tracks and bounded up the steps only seconds before the doors shut. The streetcar began its habitual rattle along the rusty tracks.

There were not many people in the car on a Sunday morning, so they had their pick of seats. Vera always liked to sit at the back, next to the window, and Aunt Isi slid into the seat beside her. Susan sat alone in the seat in front of them.

She pressed her forehead against the cool glass. When the streetcar entered a short, dark tunnel, Susan's reflection stared back at her. She frowned at her freckled nose, her heavy eyebrows and large hazel eyes, the loose curls that always escaped from her braids, her full lips. Even now, in the midst of her turmoil, she couldn't help wishing that every- thing about her was just a little less so. A little less curl and freckle and color and lips. It was Vera who had inherited the best physical qualities of both Papa and Mama.

Susan shrugged, relieved that the tunnel was short. She could now fix her gaze on the rolling hills of Buda on the far side of the Danube. The sprawling city of Budapest was split in half – into Buda and Pest – by the Danube River. The flat Pest side housed most of the city's population and businesses. While Susan had always enjoyed living in Pest, the heart of the city, with its constant hustle and bustle, she also loved looking across to Buda with its majestic castle and church steeples rising above the forested slopes.

Gellert Mountain, where they were now headed, was part of Buda's chain of hills. She had often climbed it with Papa. From the citadel at the top, he had liked to gaze down on the breathtaking view of the city. As their path wound around the statue of St. Gellert, Papa would retell the story of Gellert, the ninth-century Catholic bishop who helped convert the Hungarian people to Catholicism. But after his patron – King St. Stephen – died, the pagan "nonbelievers" seized Gellert, placed him inside a large wooden barrel, and rolled him down the hillside into the Danube River. Susan shuddered at the thought.

The hillside must have looked quite different then, without the busy street circling its base or the citadel crowning its summit. Just bare rock. Even those trees must have grown later. Her index finger traced the jagged contour of the hill on the window.

Though she and Papa had climbed the mountain several times, Susan did not remember ever seeing a convent there.

Chapter 5

Sunday Mass

Too soon for Susan, their ride was over and they continued by foot up the steep, narrow road. There were several other people heading in the same direction, all dressed in their Sunday best. Susan reached down and smoothed out her blue skirt beneath her coat. Both she and Vera wore skirts as blue as the sky in midsummer and white blouses.

"I put your new identification papers in the pockets of your jackets," Aunt Isi reminded the girls. "You are now 'legally' my nieces."

Just as Vera started to complain about her legs being tired, they arrived at the tall wrought iron fence that encircled the convent grounds. The elaborate grill gates in front of the main entrance were wide open. A majestic church, its bells pealing loudly, stood to the left, uphill from the convent building. Aunt Isabella led the girls down the wide flagstone path lined with towering chestnut trees, their bare branches rustling in the wind. Before they reached the heavily carved front doors of the convent, Aunt Isi turned them onto the side path leading toward the church.

Both Susan and Vera gasped as they stepped inside the ancient church. The vast splendor was overwhelming, yet it also had a familiar feel. "Why, it's sort of like the synagogue on Dohany Street where we went with Mama and Papa on Rosh Hashanah, the Jewish New Year, before it was all shuttered up," Susan whispered. Her eyes scanned the mas-sive marble pillars, the high ceiling, the ivory-colored walls and the deeply recessed stained glass windows. But unlike the synagogue, there were many statues here. As she looked at the seated people she

Susan and Vera were used to going to services at their Jewish synagogue.

29

noticed that men, women, and children sat together. In the synagogue, she and Vera stayed with Mama up in the balcony with the other women. From there, they had looked down on the rows and rows of bowed heads of the men. Papa's was easy to pick out because of his red hair.

The girls found the nuns' "hats" very strange.

In the church, Aunt Isi dropped to one knee, indicating with a nod of her head to Vera and Susan that they should do the same.

"It's called genuflecting," she whispered to the girls as they stood back up. "It is customary to do this every time you enter the church." They walked silently up the wide center aisle toward the front, past rows of people of all ages and sizes.

They sat down near the front, behind several rows that were filled with strangely dressed women. Vera and Susan looked at each other behind Aunt Isabella's back and grimaced. Earlier, their aunt had described the nuns. Seeing them in real life was quite different. The women on the left side of the aisle looked ordinary enough. They all wore pale gray gowns with full-length, white tunics draped over the front and back. Their hair was hidden under solid, white veils that reached halfway down their backs. Susan had occasionally seen nuns dressed like that in the city streets.

It was the women on the right-hand side who seemed strange. Their gowns were simpler, a solid black. But on their heads they had the most curious "hats." A small white cap covered their hair, and from the cap, on either side, sprouted broad, white "wings."

Susan wondered if she, too, would have to dress like that. They had brought no extra clothes with them. Aunt Isi had

Aunt Isi told the girls what to do during Mass when she took them to the convent.

said it would look suspicious if they left the house with any type of baggage.

Suddenly, everyone stood up as the priest entered. He seemed much younger than the rabbi at their synagogue. There were no wrinkles on his face. He looked out at the congregation and traced the sign of a large cross on the front of his chest.

"*In nominee Patris, et Filii, et Spiritus Sancti.*" The words of the unfamiliar language resonated above their heads.

"That is Latin," Aunt Isi whispered, "the language of the Catholic church."

Susan looked up at the vaulted, gilded ceiling, remembering the last time she had been in the synagogue on Yom Kippur, the Jewish Day of Atonement. The front of the church was very similar to the elaborate sanctuary of the synagogue with its ark, which housed the sacred Torah scrolls. *Perhaps things won't be quite so strange and different after all*, she thought for the moment.

As the service continued and the congregation sang hymns and responded in unison to statements made by the priest, Susan realized that any similarity ended at the physical level. She glanced at Vera to see if the strangeness intimidated her younger sister. But, no, as usual Vera was excited by anything new. She looked around eagerly and tugged periodically at Aunt Isi's sleeve, whispering questions. Susan closed her eyes and tried to pretend that she was in the synagogue with her Mama beside her.

The hour passed slowly. There was a final hymn, then they all stood while the priest left the sanctuary. The nuns filed out silently, not through the main doors at the back like the rest of the congregation, but rather through a smaller side door on the right side of the church. As they had agreed before entering, Aunt Isi gently guided the girls toward the nuns and then departed.

Chapter 6

Sister Agnes

As soon as Susan and Vera passed through the door into a large vestibule, they were surrounded by the nuns. Without Aunt Isi, Vera became more fearful amidst the strangers and tightly held on to Susan's hand. Though she was scared herself, Susan tried to be strong for Vera's sake. Looking resolutely into the curious faces peering at them, she noticed that there were several young girls, wearing gray tunics, among the black-clad nuns.

One face, much older than the rest, disengaged itself from the others and came up to Susan and Vera. Kindly blue eyes framed by deep wrinkles embraced the two girls.

"Hello, you must be Susan and Vera," a soft voice greeted them. "I am Mother Gabriel, the Mother Superior. I am in charge here at the

Convent of the Sisters of Charity. We are very pleased to have you with us. We will do all we can to make your stay comfortable. The other girls here are happy enough, and we hope you will be, as well." Young heads nodded energetically in agreement.

"Sister Agnes will introduce you to the other girls. She is in charge of the education of the younger girls, as well as overseeing the dormitories." Mother Gabriel straightened and beckoned to one of the nuns. "Sister Agnes, here are Susan and Vera. Please help them to get settled. They will meet the rest of our Sisters at dinner. Now, we must all go about our work."

With that, Mother Gabriel clapped her hands lightly together as a signal. The nuns and the girls turned and, without a sound, dispersed through a large wooden door that led out into the sunshine.

Sister Agnes extended both her hands warmly to Susan and Vera. "Follow me and I will show you where everything is. And most important, I will introduce you to the other girls." When she smiled, her whole face was transformed. There was something almost mischievous or conspiratorial in the sparkle of Sister Agnes's small gray eyes. Vera readily dropped Susan's hand and took hers.

"We call ourselves Sisters of Charity, because we look after the sick and poor in the city," Sister Agnes continued as they walked along the path toward the convent. "Some of the nuns go out to help people in their homes or in schools while others work here in our own school for orphans, or in the infirmary."

"Are you really all sisters?" asked Vera. "I can't imagine having so many sisters at once."

"No, we are not really sisters," smiled Sister Agnes. "Not like you and Susan. We are only sisters in spirit – in wanting to do the same things and live our lives the same way. We are followers of the order founded by St. Vincent de Paul in 1851, in France," Sister Agnes explained as they stepped through the door and slowly walked along the path. "Have you ever heard of him?"

Susan and Vera both shook their heads, no. Susan was not interested in knowing anything about the nuns, but she remained silent. She was more interested in the beautiful garden that they were walking through.

"Why are all these statues here?" asked Vera, her attention distracted by a beautifully carved, white marble statue of a woman bent over the lifeless body of the man in her arms.

"This is part of a group of statues that stand between the church and the convent." Sister Agnes pointed to the other marble forms that peeked out from among the bushes and tall trees. "See, the distance between the buildings isn't really that great, but the path winds around, up and down the hill, in order to pass by all fourteen statues. They are called the Stations of the Cross. Each statue is a reminder of an event during the time of Jesus' suffering and death."

Vera reached out her hand to feel the cold, smooth hardness of the statue.

"Are they all this sad?" she asked.

"This statue is Mary, the mother of – "

"Vera doesn't need to know about that stuff," Susan interrupted. "We are Jewish."

35

That was another promise Susan had made to Mama before their parting, one that she was confident she could keep. Mama had stressed to her the importance of always remembering her Jewish identity. "You must promise that you will never forget who you are," her mother had said. "And it will be up to you to make sure Vera also knows."

"Yes," said Sister Agnes, acknowledging Susan. "But Vera asked me a question and I felt she deserved an honest and clear answer. Besides," she added, "the man and the woman depicted in that statue, Mary and Jesus, they were Jewish, too."

Susan hoped her surprise didn't show on her face. Instead, she looked down at the bushes and barren flowerbeds lining the path.

"Those are mostly rose bushes," Sister Agnes volunteered. "The fragrance along here in the summer is heavenly."

"Roses!" Susan whispered to herself. Roses were Mama's special flowers. They were her namesake. Every Friday, before things got bad, Papa had bought a single red rose for Mama for the Sabbath. "A rose for my Rose," he always said.

"Ooh, Papa, that is so sentimental," Susan would complain, though secretly pleased that Papa loved Mama so much.

"He promised that he would give me a fresh rose every week of our lives," Mama blushingly explained one day. "He said it was a symbol of our love for each other, which would always remain fresh and beautiful." After Papa left, there were no more roses.

"Let's go see the next statue," Vera tugged at her hand, bringing her back to reality.

The sun was warmer now and the wind had died down. Susan inhaled the fresh scent of damp earth. The clouds had all dispersed. The sky above was clear and blue. It was so calm here, so different from the life of the city below. For the first time, Susan realized how seldom she and Mama had been outside since Papa had been taken away.

Chapter 7

Meeting the Girls

Susan watched Vera who had let go of her hand and skipped on ahead. Her yellow curls bobbed up and down in harmony with Sister Agnes's wings. Susan envied her little sister's light-hearted innocence, wishing for the first time that she too was still little, too little to understand what was happening in the world. But then, Sister Agnes looked happy too. Perhaps, sheltered here in this convent, she was oblivious to the hardships of city life. Susan quickened her steps to catch up to Sister Agnes and Vera, just as they entered through the solid wooden doors of the convent.

"The dormitories are up here on the second floor," explained Sister Agnes, as she led them up a wide marble stairway. Susan and Vera glanced around curiously at the massive stone pillars that adorned the entranceway and the dark corridors branching off to the left and right. "We used to look after Christian orphans here. But now they have all been sent elsewhere so that we could make room for all the Jewish girls needing our help." Sister Agnes stopped in front of the first door they came to. "Each room sleeps up to twelve girls. With you two here, we will now have almost two rooms completely full. There is a third room with only six older girls, between sixteen and eighteen, who prefer to have a room to themselves."

She knocked twice on the door and pushed it open.

"Come and meet our newcomers, girls," she called out cheerfully. A hush fell over the room as the three of them entered.

"Panni here," she began, indicating a girl with straight, black hair cut to perfectly frame her round face, "is one of the first Jewish girls who came to stay with us. Her sister, Anna, is there on the next bed," Sister Agnes began the introductions. "Panni just had her fifteenth birthday yesterday." Sister Agnes smiled at Panni, who was drawing in her new notebook as they entered. "I see you are putting your gift to work already."

Quickly, the girls scrambled off their beds and hurried over. Others came in from the adjoining room. Amidst loud bantering and jostling, everyone arranged themselves on the first couple of beds. Many of the younger girls struggled to sit next to Sister Agnes. But she reserved one spot next to her for Vera, who had managed once again to slip from Susan's side and was now snuggling up comfortably beside the nun.

Susan remained standing despite Sister Agnes's invitation to sit

One of the Guardian Angel House nuns with some of the children.

on the other side of her. She was taken aback by the smiles and light laughter, by the carefree vitality of the girls. She had anticipated tears and sorrow from girls who had been separated from their families. She looked around in confusion.

It certainly couldn't be the physical comforts that were the cause of their contentment. The long narrow room, though very clean, was also very drab. Apart from the neatly made beds, each of which was covered with a simple wool blanket and a small wooden table between every two beds, the room was bare. There wasn't even a carpet on the worn wooden floor. A large Crucifix hung from the end wall. Obviously, nobody minded. It was such a contrast to their home, where Mama's colorful paintings covered the walls.

Sister Agnes's attempts at formal introductions fizzled quickly as eager voices interrupted, volunteering some of the novel aspects of convent life.

"We have school every day, but it's more fun here."

"And we get to go outside and play every day. Sister Agnes said we can help with the garden when it gets warmer."

"We have to get up at five in the morning to go to Mass! Except for Sundays, like today. Sundays we get to sleep in till eight."

"And we say a long prayer called the Rosary, but we can each get a string of beads to hold if we want. Except it's not a necklace. Sister Agnes gets upset if we put it around our necks."

"And you can't understand anything, because it's all in a language called Latin."

"We have to help out in the kitchen."

"And clean the bathroom."

Susan gazed in wonder at the group of girls. They sounded like they enjoyed being here, despite the work and early hours. How had they so easily forgotten about the families they had left behind?

Vera showed her excitement right away. Her eyes sparkled and she bounced up and down with delight as she looked from one eager speaker to the next. Susan frowned. She was unable to push the pain-filled face of Mama at their parting out of her mind.

As if reading her thoughts, Anna, a thin girl about her own age with straight, brown hair pulled back into a tight ponytail and heavy rimmed glasses, said in a more solemn tone, "We pray for our families every day, too. All of us, including all the nuns. We worry about our families all the time." A momentary hush fell over the group as she said this. Anna's eyes locked with Susan's. She at least seemed to understand how Susan felt. Yet she, too, seemed happy.

"Why don't you tell us about your family," suggested Sister Agnes quietly. "Do you have a picture of them, Susan?"

"No," Susan's response was slow. She felt sad and ashamed of her neglect to bring a family picture with her. "There – there was no time. We left in such a rush." She bit her lower lip to keep her chin from trembling. She blinked her eyes to fight back the tears that threatened to spill onto her cheeks.

"Well you can draw us a picture then, like many of the other girls have," said Sister Agnes, her voice gentle.

Looking round the room again, Susan saw that each bed had a picture tacked to the wall beside it at pillow level. Some were photographs, others drawings. By Panni's bed was a rather good sketch. It seemed to be an imitation of the photograph beside Anna's bed, judging by the formal composition of the parents standing behind two seated, stiff-backed girls. Panni was a good artist, Susan noted with interest.

"We have a baby brother named Tomas," Vera was saying, eager to enlighten the others about their family. "Papa had to leave a long time ago to go to work. Aunt Isi said – "

"How long have you been here?" Susan interrupted, wanting to put a stop to Vera. "Why do you have all of us Jewish girls here?" She looked at Sister Agnes. "How did it all start?"

"It hasn't really been that long," Sister Agnes began, thinking back. "Panni and Anna came two, maybe three, weeks ago. As I mentioned before, they were the first Jewish girls here. Then, within days, the others came, one by one." Sister Agnes looked around at them all. "I guess none of you, besides Panni and Anna, know how it all came about. It was my brother's friend Viktor Majori who first suggested that we take in Jewish girls."

Chapter 8

A Place of Refuge

Sister Agnes explained the story. Before coming to live at the convent, she had lived a short distance from the base of Gellert Mountain with her parents and her older brother. Viktor, a high school friend of her brother, was a frequent visitor in their home, almost a part of their family. He and Agnes became friends by volunteering at community events that helped the poor and needy people of the city. Viktor was ecstatic when, after finishing school, he got a job at a local museum through the assistance of a Jewish neighbor, Mr. Dobos. He was forever grateful to Mr. Dobos for that.

"After I joined the convent," Sister Agnes explained, "Viktor came to visit occasionally, perhaps two or three times a year, on one of the many feast days. Whenever he came, Viktor brought donations of food and clothing, news of past friends, and of the growing problems in the world.

"Viktor's visit was unexpected in the middle of February with no major feast day approaching. He came alone and, for the first time, empty-handed. The day was overcast, cold and windy, so we remained in the large foyer. I sat on a wooden bench, while Viktor paced back and forth in front me, clearly upset.

"'The people in this country are acting insane,' he said. 'They seem to be forgetting how to be human. The hostility against Jewish people is reaching new heights. You must have heard about it even here.' Then he continued without waiting for my reply.

"'You remember Mr. Dobos," he asked, 'the man who helped me get my job at the museum? Well, I entered his office the other day, eager to tell him about a new shipment that had just arrived. And there he was, sitting with his elbows on his desk, his head in his hands, a picture of his wife and two daughters in front of him. When he lifted his head, there were tears running down his cheeks. I asked what the matter was. He told me that he was very worried about his family, that he didn't know how to protect them anymore. Last week when his wife went to buy a new winter coat for their youngest daughter, a customer in the store just looked at them and stomped out. Then a couple of days ago, the woman working in the grocery store told her to go shop elsewhere – they weren't serving Jews anymore. His wife had shopped there for years! How could that woman speak to her like that?'" Sister Agnes paused and looked at Panni and Anna. They nodded in agreement.

"Yes it happened just like that," said Panni. "My mother was so upset when she came home. She had cooked meals for that shop owner when she was sick in bed, and now she wouldn't sell anything to my mother because she was Jewish."

Looking round, Susan noticed that other girls were nodding their heads, too. They were all familiar with this kind of story. For the first time, listening to this animated and heartfelt account, Susan began to appreciate her mother's desperation in sending them to the convent.

"Even at the museum, where Mr. Dobos had worked for years, he was no longer treated well," Sister Agnes continued. "He was practically ignored. The janitor wouldn't even clean his office anymore. And then, the night before Viktor came to the convent, soldiers came to the building next to the one where Mr. Dobos lived and took several Jewish men with them. They were being sent to labor camps. Mr. Dobos was worried that he might be taken next, or that he might lose his job. How would his family survive?

"'I can't stand by and do nothing.' Viktor told me."

Sister Agnes paused to shift Vera, who had fallen asleep with her head in her lap, into a more comfortable position. Then she went on.

"Viktor stopped in front of me. He knelt down and gripped my arms. He had an idea, he said. It was a crazy idea, he admitted, and it might not be possible, but he had to try. He couldn't stand by anymore and see his mentor so distraught over the future of his girls. In a way, he frightened me. I had never seen such intensity in Viktor's eyes or heard his voice so desperate.

"'I thought…' began Viktor, 'I thought that perhaps his daughters could come here to the convent. There are so many girls here. A couple more or less would not make that much difference. They could pretend to be orphans, or young novices. No one would dream of looking for Jewish girls here. Everyone in the country needs identity papers now. But no one would come here asking for identity papers. Not in a convent.'"

"At first, I didn't know what to say," continued Sister Agnes. We nuns have always responded by opening our doors wide to those in need. We have always believed in overcoming hardships for the sake of serving others. But we have never been asked to do anything like this – something in secret."

Sister Agnes's voice took on a new energy as she spoke. As if she was trying to impress upon them the weight of her dilemma. All the eyes focused on her, Susan noted, were filled with understanding. Many of them, though so much younger than the nun, had already faced similar situations. Though they all knew the outcome of her story, they waited breathlessly for her to continue.

"I told Victor that I would speak to Mother Gabriel and that he should come back in a few days for a decision. But Victor was adamant. 'No! A few days might be too late. I must speak with the Mother Superior now!'

"I went in search of Mother Gabriel. I had always admired her wisdom, but it was only after that day that I also learned to appreciate her foresight. As she listened to Viktor re-tell his story, her face gradually transformed from initial dismay to quiet determination. 'You understand,' Mother Gabriel said gravely to Viktor when he finished, 'that in accepting these two girls, we will be accepting many. For if we allow two, how can we say no to the rest? We cannot ignore the suffering of others.'

"She pointed out to him the danger of what he was asking us to do, both to himself and our community. But then she thanked him for his request and agreed to honor it.

"With her decision made, things moved quickly. All the Christian orphans, who were not in danger from the Nazis, were placed in foster homes or sent to other houses run by our Sisters. Just over a week after Viktor's visit, Panni and Anna arrived."

"And it has been wonderful living here," said Anna, looking right at Susan. "For the first time since I can remember, I only see friendly faces around me. I just wish we didn't have to get up so early for Mass during the week," she added.

"Yes, I know that there are things that are difficult to get used to at first," said Sister Agnes. "But Mother Gabriel has also stressed that for appearance sake, just in case anyone notices, the Jewish girls must participate in all the activities of the convent. We must carry on as we always have. However, she also said that all of us nuns must show the utmost respect for your Jewish faith and customs. We will strive to live here as one family."

Chapter 9

Together and Alone

The clanging of a loud bell put a sudden stop to Sister Agnes's story.

"Oh dear, I haven't even shown you where you'll be sleeping yet, and it's already lunch time," she exclaimed as the girls scrambled off the beds.

"Here, follow me quickly," Sister Agnes said as they hurried ahead toward the back of the long, narrow room of beds. "You will be over here on this side, Vera, next to Irene, who is just a year older than you. And your sister will be on your other side. I assume you two sisters will want to stay together, right?"

She stopped about three-quarters of the way down the right side, in front of two beds identical to all the others in the room. "There's room for only two more girls in this room after you. We'll have to open up another dormitory if more girls come. You can leave your jackets here for now," she said, indicating the foot of the beds. "It will help you recognize your beds when you come back tonight."

They hurried back to the doorway where the other girls were already assembled. "You are all wonderful for waiting so patiently," Sister Agnes's grateful smile encompassed the entire group. Susan hurried to keep up with the group of girls who followed Sister Agnes along the marble hallway. As they turned a corner and descended a set of stairs, Anna fell in step beside her.

"This place is enormous, isn't it?" she said, echoing Susan's own thoughts. "At first I was scared of getting lost, but I've learned where everything is now."

Anna gave Susan a detailed description of the layout of the convent. It was actually very simple, she explained. The building was a large rectangle, split in half by the set of stairs they were descending. The ground floor they were heading toward contained the lounge, a library, and some offices on one side of the stairs. The kitchen, dining room, and laundry were on the other side. The first floor had the dormitories and classrooms, again divided by the stairs, and the top floor contained all the nuns' rooms. There were stairs at either end of the building as well, with doors leading to the outside.

"Oh, and there are also doors leading into the back garden, one from the center stairwell and one from the kitchen," Anna added. "But the kitchen is off limits to us unless you are assigned work duty there."

"Work duty?" Susan asked. But Anna seemed not to have heard her. She adjusted her glasses, which had slipped down her nose, and gave Susan a sideways glance.

"I love the color of your hair," she said self consciously, changing the subject. "It's not drab like mine. It makes you stand out. Though I suppose you're not crazy about the freckles that go with it. I hate my freckles and I don't have nearly as many as you." Susan, who was normally very sensitive about any comments regarding the color of her hair and freckles, couldn't help but laugh at Anna's honesty.

As they approached the dining room, their steps slowed and the group of girls entered sedately through the large double doors. Nuns were streaming in from other directions.

"We sit over here," Anna nudged her and, taking her hand, led her toward one of the long wooden tables where several of the girls were already standing behind their wooden chairs. Susan noticed Vera at the next table in animated conversation with three other girls.

"You're lucky you arrived on a Sunday," Anna was saying to her. "On Sundays we are allowed to talk during meals. On the other days, we must keep silent while one of the nuns reads aloud from their Bible. At lunch time they read from the Old Testament and at supper from *The Lives of Saints*. Many of the readings are strange and hard to understand, or simply boring. But some are actually interesting. I like the ones about a St. Francis. He lived outside and was friends with the birds and animals."

"*Benedic, Domine, nos et haec tua…*"

"That's the blessing we say before all the meals. They say all their prayers in Latin, like we say ours in Hebrew." Anna whispered.

"On Friday night, our Jewish Sabbath, Mother Gabriel always asks one of the older girls to say our prayer in Hebrew," another girl added. There was a loud shuffling of chairs as everyone sat down.

From another doorway, several girls entered carrying plates of steaming food.

"Those are the older girls," Anna whispered again. "We all take turns helping in the kitchen and dining room. On Sundays, they and Mother Gabriel serve the rest of us. She says it's so we can practice the spirit of service." Sure enough, there was Mother Gabriel, also emerging through the kitchen door, balancing two full plates in each hand.

But it was the girl who came out directly behind Mother Gabriel that held Susan's attention. "Julia!" Susan mouthed silently as she recognized her cousin. The small, slender girl, with a proud bearing that gave the illusion that she was much taller than she was, came straight over to their table and placed the plates of roast chicken, boiled potatoes, and carrots down at the far end. She turned her head. Her dark eyes swept by Susan, came back, and locked with hers in recognition. The intensity of that look, a combination of surprise and distance, confused Susan, and she turned away, saying nothing in greeting.

"The food is very plain, but at least we have something to eat," Anna was saying. "We never had enough when we were at home. Some days we only ate bread and clear soup."

After Sunday lunch, it was free time for the girls. Susan shuffled her feet along the white stone path in the garden. The nuns were praying, and Susan, unaccustomed to being surrounded by so many people, was glad to escape by herself. Also, she wanted to figure out how her cousin Julia came to be here at the convent. Certainly her mother would not have known, or she would have said something to Susan.

In the garden, the ground beneath her feet was hard and bare, but here and there, patches of grass were beginning to turn green. Spring was on its way. She heard faint snatches of conversation and childish giggles floating in the air around her. She caught glimpses of grey-clad forms moving between the clusters of bushes and towering trees. The garden was so large that even with all these people here she could be alone. It was an aloneness she didn't mind.

Wandering up the hill toward the back end of the garden, she came upon a large fallen log, sheltered by an overhanging bush. She sat down on the ground, and after adjusting herself into a comfortable position, she pulled from her pocket the pad of paper and pencil that Sister Agnes had given to her after lunch. "It's for the picture of your family," Sister Agnes had explained briefly before hurrying off.

Susan chewed on the end of her pencil. She had no eraser, and her pad had only a few sheets of paper. She couldn't afford to make too many mistakes. She thought of the drawing she had seen earlier by Panni's bed, the careful reproduction of the photograph beside Anna's bed.

I could never draw a picture like that, she thought. *In drawing or painting, you eventually have to find your own way,* Mama's words whispered in her mind. Mama was such a good artist!

"I'm so happy that you're an artist, too," her mother had exclaimed years ago, when Susan had shown her a drawing that she was proud of. "See how you naturally use all the space on the paper – it shows you have an eye for composition and design. And your lines are great." Since that day, Mama had encouraged and guided her passion for drawing.

I'm no good at portraits, mused Susan, *so it's no use wasting paper on trying to do that.* She closed her eyes trying to recall her favorite image of Papa and Mama. Finally, she settled on doing two separate pictures. One was of Mama angled from behind, showing her back and just a hint of the outline of her face. In the picture, Mama stood by the window overlooking the courtyard, holding back the curtains, looking out for Papa to come home. The other picture was of Papa leaning against the wall, cradling the newly born Tomas in his arms, his head tilted in attentive listening.

Once she had the images clearly in her mind, Susan's pencil flew over the paper. When she had the basic forms down, she slowed, concentrating on adding the finer details of shadows and lines. As she worked, she felt strangely close to Mama, almost hearing her gentle suggestions in her ear: *Remember to make the shading darker near the edges of your shapes… Yes, just a few lines are enough to give a sense of Papa's curls.* She took a deep breath, straightened her back, put her papers and pencil back in her pocket, and looked around her. She felt refreshed and at peace, surprised that while she drew, she so easily forgot her worries. So it was a shock when she heard a vaguely familiar voice call her name.

"Susan!" She turned and looked into her cousin Julia's face.

Chapter 10

Julia

Even though they were second cousins and had lived only blocks from each other, Susan wasn't really close to Julia. When they had met at noisy family gatherings or passed each other in the street, Julia, almost four years older, tended to ignore Susan, preferring the company of older cousins or adults.

The main thing Susan knew about Julia was that she sang. Everybody in the family always talked about what an exceptional voice she had. She had been taking lessons for years and sometimes performed. She had sung in a musical and at a few special events in the city.

Susan had overheard her parents talking about how it had all come to a sudden stop. Julia was forced to quit her voice lessons. Some parents had complained about their children having to sing with a Jewish girl. The teacher said she could not afford to lose clients because of her. Besides, Jews were no longer allowed to perform publicly, so the teacher figured it was a waste of her efforts training Julia.

"It's such a shame," Papa had said shaking his head. "Julia has incredible talent and apparently she is very angry at the injustice of it all."

Shortly after that, Papa left and Susan didn't hear anything more about Julia for a long time. Then one day, she and Mama were shopping in the market when they ran into her Aunt Margaret, Julia's mother.

"Julia has become very rebellious and has started to hang out with the older boys," Aunt Margaret complained to Mama. "With high school suspended for Jews and no singing lessons, she has too much time on her hands. Ferenc suspects that she is helping in the underground resistance efforts – forging documents to help Jews leave the country. But she is clever enough that even we can't pinpoint exactly what she is doing and when." Aunt Margaret shook her head. "Ferenc is very concerned that she will get into trouble."

"What a worry it must be for you and Ferenc!" Mama had sympathized. "Definitely an extra burden that you don't need."

Then, in the midst of Mama's deliberation about sending Susan and Vera to the convent, Susan overheard a conversation between Aunt Isi and Mama.

"I ran into Margaret at the bakery today," Mama had said quietly. "I asked after the family. She said Ferenc, too, was ordered to work in a labor camp. And Julia, well, Ferenc sent Julia into hiding just days before he left. So thankfully, she doesn't know that he is gone. I suspect they found a safe place for her. Of course, I didn't ask where or how. It isn't prudent. We can't endanger anyone or each other by saying too much. The less we know the less we can reveal if questioned."

"How did *you* come to the convent?" Julia now asked her. Susan shrugged, hoping to appear indifferent and mature.

"Aunt Isi arranged it. It all happened so quickly, I don't know all the details."

"Who is Aunt Isi?" Julia looked puzzled.

"She's Mama's friend from high school. How did *you* get here?"

"My father got me false identification papers that said I was born and baptized Catholic." Julia scowled and to Susan's horror she spit on the ground. "'It's for your own good. We want you to be safe, dear.'" Julia mimicked her father's voice perfectly. She flung her thick, shoulder-length hair behind her and batted her heavy lashes at Susan. "Well I don't want to be safe. I want to help in the Underground. Papa doesn't realize how much we did, the boys and I." Julia's voice was tinged with anger and resentment. She paused, lost momentarily in her memories. A vague smile flickered on her face.

"Weren't you ever frightened?" asked Susan. "Weren't you scared of getting caught?"

"There is no time to be frightened when you focus on helping others," Julia answered. "That was all we thought about: helping others and resisting the injustice we all suffered. We stole and altered identity papers for those who really needed them. We stole food cards for families who didn't have enough. They needed me." Again, Julia's eyes had that faraway look as she recalled her adventures. Next to her, Susan felt like a little girl, younger than her eleven years.

"I could get into some places easier because I was smaller and sometimes because I was a girl," Julia continued. "People didn't suspect me. I can look very innocent when I want."

"When did you come here?" asked Susan.

"I've been here nearly three weeks now," Julia replied. "I was so angry with Papa when he left, I didn't even say goodbye. Why couldn't he see the good I was doing?"

Suddenly, Susan realized that Julia still did not know about her father having been sent to the labor camp. "Julia – " Susan began, just as a bell rang out three times in succession. She had no time to finish her sentence.

"Catechism time," Julia interrupted her. "It isn't so bad. Mother Gabriel leads it on Sundays and it is about the life of Jesus. She always tells it like a story. If you close your eyes and listen, you can almost see the desert sands where Jesus walked. I wonder what Jerusalem is really like? It's supposed to be our promised land, but I wonder if we will ever set foot there. Come on. It's very bad if we're late. 'Punctuality is a virtue' Sister Agnes always reminds us." Again, Julia's voice mimicked Sister Agnes's perfectly. Susan giggled.

"I didn't know you could do that," she said admiringly. "You know, imitate people like that."

"Well not many people do know, so don't say anything. And nobody here knows I sing, either," Julia added. "So keep your mouth shut about that. I'm not interested in performing anymore."

They had come to the path that led to the back door of the convent and were joined by other hurrying feet.

Susan forgot to mention about Uncle Ferenc being sent to the labor camp.

Chapter 11
Daily Routine

Susan opened her eyes reluctantly. Total blackness surrounded her. Somewhere a bell rang. It took her several moments to recollect where she was. Someone turned on the lights.

"Hey, what's going on?" she started to ask, but remembered that Anna had explained the night before that every morning they rose at 5:00 am for Mass.

"Don't they have Mass only on Sundays?" Susan had asked, worried about getting up so early every morning.

"That's when most Catholics go to Mass. But these nuns start every day with it," Anna replied, rolling her eyes at the confusing logic of it all.

Beside her, Vera was still curled in a tight ball, sound asleep. Susan smiled down at her little sister. It was only at bedtime last night that Vera first missed Mama. Susan, hearing her quiet whimpering, had slipped out of bed and climbed in next to her.

"I'm glad to see you two can comfort each other," Sister Agnes said when she passed by on her nightly rounds. "I know you must miss your parents very much." The nun knelt down beside the bed and laid her hand gently on Susan's shoulder. "It is good to miss them. It shows how much you love them. I am so glad you are here where we can take care of you so that your Mama can know you are safe." Sister Agnes's words sent a warm glow through Susan and she fell asleep with her arms wrapped around Vera.

After a few attempts at rousing her sister, Susan gave up. This was much too early for Vera. *They won't notice one person missing*, she hoped.

Susan pulled the gray tunic she was given the previous night over her head. Sluggishly, she followed the other girls to the dormitory door. Sister Agnes was there waiting for them, mouthing their names as they walked by her. As Susan passed, Sister Agnes raised a questioning eyebrow. Susan shrugged her shoulder. To her relief, Sister Agnes let her pass without a word.

Silently the girls stepped into the chill air of the sleeping garden. The full moon was high overhead. Somewhere a bird released a high melodious call: "Pee-tee, pee-tee, pee-tee." There was a moment of complete silence and then it began again. Another moment of silence and another bird joined in – and then another. By the time they reached the church, an entire symphony of chirps and trills accompanied them.

In the church, Susan sat, stood, and knelt mechanically, trying to remain conscious enough to follow the actions of the others. Thankfully, the weekday service was much shorter than the full hour of the previous morning.

On their return, Susan found Vera still sound asleep. This time she had no choice but to wake her. All the beds had to be neatly made, everything put in order, the room swept and mopped before they could all hurry to the dining room for breakfast.

The blended aroma of freshly brewed coffee, hot cocoa, and yeast rolls greeted their nostrils and growling stomachs as they neared the dining room. Vera squeezed Susan's hand and smiled up at her in eager anticipation. Susan recalled their breakfasts at home: weak tea and stale bread spread, with a very thin layer of raspberry jam. If only Mama could share this meal with them.

Immediately after breakfast, each of the girls was assigned to one of the nuns to help with their particular task. Vera and Irene went with Sister Agnes to get the classroom ready for the day's lessons. Susan was delegated to the laundry room.

The hour spent rinsing tunics in front of a long line of laundry tubs passed quickly. As the nuns and girls sloshed and scrubbed the clothes in their steaming tub, they sang. Their arms moved up and down in rhythm to the melody, their hips swayed. The songs they sang were children's lullabies and familiar folk songs, not the religious hymns Susan would have expected.

By nine o'clock, all the girls were ready for class. Breakfast dishes had been cleared away and washed, and most of the convent had been swept, scrubbed, and aired out. In the classroom, Sister Agnes directed the activities with another nun assisting as needed.

"We don't have actual grades," Anna explained. "Sister Agnes says there are too few of us in each grade to worry about where one begins and another ends. Plus, there are new people like you and Vera coming here every day." Anna shook her head with the confusion of it all. "Anyhow," she continued, adjusting her glasses, "we just carry on from wherever we left off the last time we were in school. Sister Agnes and Sister Teresa walk around helping us when we need them." Together they went to the back of the class to collect their books.

"Here, we can push our desks together and help each other. We are probably at the same level," Anna offered.

Susan gazed around the large room after they sat down. It looked like a regular classroom with its rows of tables and chairs, the large blackboard at the front, and a faded globe of the world on a pedestal in one corner. Yet it was so different from the school she had attended! Here, everyone belonged. Heads bent together in quiet, friendly conversation, the nuns helping everyone with equal willingness.

She and Vera had not attended school for the last few weeks. Because they were Jewish, their teachers had ignored them. They were never asked to answer questions. Their raised hands were unheeded.

They were moved to the back of the class, their papers unmarked. Mama, too frightened to complain, decided simply to keep them at home. For the first time in a long time, Susan settled down to her studies.

At 11:30 sharp, Sister Agnes asked all the girls to put their books away and go to their assigned mid-day duties.

"Kitchen duty is my favorite job," Anna told Susan as they hurried toward the kitchen. "There is always something to nibble on. In fact, Sister Magda insists we sample just about everything she makes, just to make sure it's okay."

Already Susan was getting used to the strictly kept routine. All the girls and those nuns who didn't have specific areas of expertise were assigned jobs for different parts of the day. Each lasted for the week, and then switched. The schedule was posted on the back of the dormitory door and on the large wooden board by the dining room. Everybody seemed to know where they were supposed to be and what to do.

A blanket of steamy warm air and a bustle of noise and activity greeted the girls as they stepped through the kitchen door. Several nuns and novices bent over large, bubbling pots on two separate coal stoves. Others stood along counters, chopping and slicing an assortment of vegetables. One nun was mixing a vast quantity of dough in an enormous bowl. Sweat trickled down her face from beneath her winged headdress. Sister Magda, a large, rosy-cheeked nun who was in charge of the kitchen, scurried from one person to the next, giving orders and tasting from the various pots.

"I'm glad you're here," she said on seeing Susan and Anna. "Come this way. You can help Ester and Julia. I was worried they wouldn't finish in time for lunch." She led them to a large wooden table off to one side where Julia and Ester were busily working with their sleeves rolled up. Ester was peeling a large red apple and Julia was deftly chopping up a skinless one on a large wooden cutting board.

"Mrs. Szabo, our neighbor from next door, brought these by." Sister Magda explained. "The Szabos are always helping us out, bless them." She shook her head and hurried back to the pots.

"Anna, you peel and, Susan, you put the pieces I cut into this bowl," Julia instructed them without looking up, indicating the bowl with a nod of her head. Susan glanced at Julia in surprise. Ester was the older of the two, but Julia was clearly the one in charge. The girls set to work.

There was no singing here. The various tasks demanded too much attention. Yet Susan could see why this was Anna's favorite place to work. There was a steady background hum of simmering food, rattling pots, crackling fire. Strings of dried red peppers, braids of garlic, and even links of sausage hung from the ceiling. The tantalizing aromas swirled around them.

"Do we actually eat all this for one meal?" Susan said in awe.

"It's not all for us," explained Ester. "Many of the nuns go outside each day to look after sick or poor people. They come back here to collect the noonday meal, then take it back to those in need. Lots of hungry people come here asking for food, too. The nuns never turn anyone away." She sighed heavily.

Susan looked at Ester more closely. She was a tall slender girl with thick brown hair that hung in a long heavy braid down her back. Her light blue eyes and narrow, colorless lips blended in with her pale face.

When Ester bent down to select another piece of fruit to peel, Anna leaned over and whispered to Susan. "Ester is always sighing like that. She has a boyfriend, but he is in a labor camp." Sure enough, when Ester's head re-emerged above the table top, she sighed again, her shoulders rising and falling before she resumed her peeling.

Suddenly, the kitchen doors opened and a group of nuns hurried in with large straw baskets hanging over their arms. They filled the baskets with prepared canisters of stuffed cabbage, hot biscuits wrapped in white cloth, and sealed containers of fresh fruit salad. Amidst the clatter and confusion, the nuns exchanged bits of local news while collecting the appropriate items. Sister Magda was everywhere at once, her "wings" bobbing up and down as she worried that something would be spilled or forgotten.

"She does this every day and nothing ever goes wrong," Anna laughed quietly as the girls stood back and watched.

"Let's get out of here before she thinks of something else for us to do. I'm starving," Julia said as they finished dicing the last apple.

The silent, calm order of the dining room was a sharp contrast to the bustling kitchen. Sister Greta's voice, as she read from the Old

Testament, rose over the faint clatter of knives and forks and the occa-sional whispered request for a dish of food or the salt to be passed. Susan felt her body relax as she took her seat, picked up her fork, and leaned back, grateful for the routine of the convent.

Part Two
Nazi Invasion

Chapter 12

The Invasion

March 19, 1944

Susan had looked forward to this day, her second Sunday at the convent. It was a chance to sleep an extra couple of hours before the later Mass at ten a.m. Perhaps she would see Aunt Isi at church. Aunt Isi had said she would try to visit the girls at Mass and perhaps even slip them a note from Mama.

But when she arrived at the church, Susan saw that there were fewer people from the surrounding area. No matter how hard she strained to see their faces, she caught no sight of her aunt. Still, she looked forward to it being Sunday with lots more time to herself. She wanted to further explore the convent and its grounds and also draw some pictures for Mama of their new surroundings.

It was disappointing, therefore, when, just after their noon meal,

Mother Gabriel asked everyone to stay behind for an important meeting, an unusual disruption of the convent's routine. Susan followed the stream of chattering girls toward the living room.

"Do you think that maybe we will get to go home?" asked Anna. Susan looked at the grim face of Sister Agnes and shook her head. She suspected that whatever Mother Gabriel had to tell them, it would not be welcome news. In the dining room, she had observed the whisperings and glances of several of the nuns. They had looked worried.

"We'll find out soon enough," she said to Anna, hoping that her premonition was wrong. They pushed through the wide double doors of the living room, hurrying to their favorite seats.

Worn but serviceable couches, easy chairs, and large cushions were arranged in conversational groupings around the room. Low wooden tables laden with coffee urns and small espresso cups, large hampers of yarn speared with knitting needles, and stacks of books were scattered here and there, giving the room a comfortable lived-in atmosphere. The walls displayed paintings of flower arrangements and bowls of colorful fruit. Heavy brocade curtains framed the tall windows that looked out onto the peaceful garden. Susan especially liked the crimson and yellow tulips planted in rustic clay pots that brightened the room.

The tinkling of Mother Gabriel's small bell ended the girls' conversations. It was the Mother Superior's signal that she wanted their attention. She nodded at one of the nuns, who promptly herded Vera and a small group of young children out to an adjoining room for a story.

Then, in a grave voice, Mother Gabriel addressed the older girls. "This morning the Germans invaded our country. Their troops have filled the streets of Budapest and our top government officials have been taken as prisoners. Apparently the Nazis grew tired of waiting for our leaders to 'deal properly' with the large Jewish population living here." Mother Gabriel paused as she looked around with concern at the girls in her charge.

A heavy, somber silence descended on the room. Gradually, as the implications of Mother Gabriel's words sank in, teary sniffles and exclamations of dismay floated around the room. They had all expected this. Susan knew that this was why their parents had hidden them here. Still, the Nazi invasion was a hard reality to face.

"I know you are all concerned about your families in the city and want to know what is going on." Mother Gabriel gazed into each of their eyes. "When I receive any further news, whether it is good or bad, I promise I will let you know immediately."

"What will the Nazis do?" Panni called out. Her question set the whole room abuzz with speculation. What new hardships would they face? And how much safer were they here than in the outside world? Susan and Anna huddled together silently, listening to the turmoil around them.

It was the return of Vera and the other little girls that restored order to the room. They had finished their story and came back, eager to join in the usual light-hearted games and conversation in the living room. For their sake, everyone forced their attention away from the disturbing news. With time, these younger children would have to be told a gentler version of what was happening.

Over the next few days, Susan became more appreciative of the firm routine of work, study, and prayer. She realized how much it helped maintain a sense of calm and focus. There were hungry mouths to feed, dirty clothes to wash, lessons to learn, and the younger children to entertain.

True to her word, Mother Gabriel shared information with the older girls as it came. On Friday morning, she told them that a new government had been established in Hungary. It was made up of Hungarians who were strong Nazi supporters. When the nuns returned from the city, where they dropped off their meals for needy families, they spoke of the large number of Nazi soldiers patrolling the streets.

The anxiety in all their hearts flared up again. Susan's thoughts turned to Mama and Tomas. She worried about their daily lives in the Nazi occupied city – and even about their survival. More than ever, she wished she could be home helping Mama.

But here she was in a convent, away from home – and she needed to do something here that would make a difference. Building up courage for her unusual request, she approached Sister Agnes. "Today is Friday," Susan said boldly. "Tonight at sundown is the beginning of our Jewish Sabbath. At home, my Mama always lit candles and we had a special meal." She swallowed in an attempt to still the sudden trembling of her voice at the memory. "Could we light candles here tonight? Could we say the Hebrew blessings? I think it would help everyone." Her eyes searched the room. "Perhaps Ester could light the candles. She is the oldest."

The nun regarded her thoughtfully. "Your Sabbath, like our Sunday, is a day of rest and peace," she said. "This might be a good idea. I will ask Mother Gabriel for her permission."

In the meantime, Susan approached Ester. "Oh, I never dreamt that we could light Sabbath candles here in the convent," exclaimed Ester, clapping her hands together. It was the first time Susan saw Ester's eyes sparkle. "I've been so worried that I will forget our Jewish traditions here. I even brought this prayer book with me to help me remember." She reached into the deep pocket of her tunic and pulled out a small, soft leather-bound book. "All the blessings and prayers of the Sabbath and holidays are in here, in Hebrew and Hungarian."

Later that evening, with her long hair covered loosely by a lace kerchief, Ester lit the two candles on the table in front of her. A hush fell over the room. Then, with her eyes closed, her hands gently circled the candles and brought them back toward her face three times, drawing the light of the candles inward. With her eyes still closed, she uttered the Hebrew blessing over the candles: "*Barukh ata adonai, eloheinu melekh ha-olam....*"

Watching Ester, Susan's eyes filled with tears. She wondered if her mother – if all their mothers – were saying these words at this very moment. She looked around at all the glistening eyes and solemn expressions. She felt the calm settle around them as the candles burned in a brief oasis of peace.

Chapter 13

Surrounded

March 28, 1944

In her sleep, Susan felt the steady rumbling. *It's the boots. They're coming to get Papa.* She sat up and rubbed her eyes, her heart pounding in her chest. No, it couldn't be. She was at the convent and Papa had been gone a long time. She climbed out of bed and groped her way to one of the windows.

With her head pressed against the cold pane of glass, she peered across the treetops to the street. A convoy of tanks, trucks, and marching soldiers was making its way laboriously up the mountainside. The thin sliver of the waning moon spread a faint light over the scene. Occasionally it lit upon the large white circle with a black swastika in the center that was displayed on the sides of the vehicles and armbands of the soldiers. Nazis! Why were they coming here to Gellert Mountain?

Then, she remembered the citadel, high above them, with its strong stone walls and ancient cannons. From there you could see the entire city of Budapest. The Nazi army would be able to see the approach of any attackers, whether by air, land, or the river. The stone walls would offer protection to the Nazi soldiers if they needed to fire at the enemy.

One by one, other girls awakened by the noise joined Susan at the window. Shivering with cold and fear, they solemnly watched the slow procession. An hour later, as they made their way to Mass, the nuns' whisperings confirmed Susan's suspicion. The Nazis were on their way to the citadel at the top of the mountain.

Throughout the next few days, the convent was surrounded by Nazis. Not only was an army base established on top of Gellert Mountain, but headquarters were set up next door to the convent building in Mr. and Mrs. Szabo's house. They were told to move elsewhere and were given a day to gather their belongings. Now, soldiers patrolled the length of the street in front of their house and the convent throughout the day.

These new developments disturbed everyone. The singing in the laundry room was replaced by worried whisperings. In the kitchen, Sister Magda became unusually quiet, forgetting to taste the simmering goulash and over-salting the soup. Mother Gabriel restricted the Jewish girls' outdoor activities to the private gardens behind the convent, away from prying eyes.

Susan recorded these changes in her drawings. She had gotten into the habit of carrying a pad of paper and pencil with her everywhere. The deep pockets of the tunics they wore were very convenient for this. Whenever she had the chance, she pulled her pad out and made a quick sketch of whatever was going on around her.

Everyone wondered what the Nazis would do next. Then, two days later, they got their answer.

Chapter 14

New Laws

March 31, 1944

The girls had just finished lighting the Sabbath candles – now a weekly event. They assembled in the living room for their evening meeting and relaxation. Mother Gabriel waited for them with the daily newspaper spread open on her lap.

As she had promised, the Mother Superior passed on all the new information to the older girls. When the room had quieted down, she read the headlines: *Jews cannot own property! All Jews must wear a yellow star. All Jews must live in designated Jewish buildings. Jews cannot hold government jobs.*

Though Hungarian Jews had been shunned and mistreated in the past, it had never been the law – not until now. The list of restrictions continued: *Jews cannot own vehicles. Jews cannot ride bicycles. Anyone*

Kathy Clark

Aprilis 5-től a zsidók sárga csillagot kötelesek viselni a házon kívül

A Hungarian newspaper article outlining the new restrictions. The headline reads "From April 5th, all Jews must wear a yellow star when outside their homes."

hiding or helping Jews will automatically go to prison.

This last law gave the girls a jolt. "Does this mean you must send us away, so that you don't have to go to prison?" Anna's voice rose above the shocked murmurings in the room. She spoke directly to the Mother Superior.

Anna is right, Susan thought. *These nuns are endangering their own lives by having us here. They will be forced to send us away.* Susan was suddenly frightened. She turned toward Mother Gabriel, holding her breath. The room was filled with tension as they all waited for her response.

Mother Gabriel scanned their faces, then finding Anna's, she smiled at her. "No, my child, we will not send you away. We will take care of all of you, until your families are ready to take you back. There may be dangers, but we will always strive to keep you safe." Several girls let out a sigh of relief.

Mother Gabriel held up her hand and raised her voice slightly to get their attention again. "Our good friend Victor Majori has come to our assistance. He managed to arrange for our convent to come under the protection of the Swedish government. The Swedes are a neutral country in this war. They haven't taken sides against or with any other country. Being under their protection means that the Nazis cannot harm us or interfere with us." She beamed back at the suddenly smiling faces that turned toward her. "A sign will be posted on the gates of the convent tomorrow announcing this. I also have special protection documents for all the Sisters residing here."

Mother Gabriel held up a piece of paper with an official looking red seal in the bottom right corner. "You must carry these with you, my daughters, whenever you leave the convent," she told the nuns. "Please come and collect them from my office before you retire tonight."

Susan could hear everyone's sigh of relief as Mother Gabriel finished. Here at the convent, they faced no immediate danger.

The respite following Mother Gabriel's last words was brief, as the girls realized the broader implications of the newspaper headlines. Susan thought of Mama and little Tomas alone in the apartment. Were they all right? Would Aunt Isi be able to protect them, or would they have to move to a "designated" building – a building marked by a large yellow star on the outside where only Jewish people were allowed to live? How will we ever get back together if they move somewhere else? The questions spun round and round in Susan's mind.

"What do you think will happen to our parents?" Julia's voice suddenly echoed her thoughts. She had come over and was sitting on the arm of Susan's easy chair. Her loose, brown hair brushed against Susan's face. "Do you think the Nazis will find out they sent us here? Do you think they will be in extra trouble?" Her brows creased with worry.

"Julia," Susan confessed, "I didn't get a chance to tell you the other day. I overheard my Mama tell Aunt Isi that your Papa was also sent away to a labor camp. It must have happened right after you came here. I – I'm sorry," she broke off as she noticed Julia's face turn pale.

"Mama is alone?" Julia exclaimed. Then, in the next instant, she buried her face in her hands. "Oh, poor Papa," she whispered to herself.

Hesitating, Susan placed her hand on Julia's back. She felt awkward trying to comfort her older cousin. But in a way Julia's distress was her fault. She should have told her before. All this bad news at once was too much to bear.

Julia turned back to Susan. "Do you know where he was sent? Have you heard anything about how he's doing?" Susan didn't have an answer.

"I was so horrible to Papa the day he brought me here," Julia went on, speaking more to herself than to Susan. "I told him I hated him for making me leave. And now I might never see him again." She moved away from Susan and whispered to herself, "I'm so sorry, Papa, for what I said to you," Julia whispered. "I do love you."

The next morning, when the girls rose, Julia was gone.

Chapter 15
Missing

Three new girls came to the convent that night, another four the following afternoon. In all the commotion over the new arrivals, it was easy for the nuns to divert the girls' attention from Julia's sudden disappearance. But after breakfast, Mother Gabriel called Susan, Anna, and Ester aside.

"Susan, you are Julia's cousin and, from what I've seen, you have become good friends with Anna." Her kind smile embraced both girls. "I figured you two would share all your thoughts and worries. And Ester," she said, looking up at the tall girl behind them, "you have become a close friend of Julia. I believe the three of you would want to know where Julia is." Mother Gabriel bit her lower lip thoughtfully, as if uncertain how to continue. The three girls glanced at each other.

It was unusual to see Mother Gabriel at a loss for words.

"The problem is that I'm afraid we don't really know," she continued at last. "I suspect that after hearing the news last night she simply ran away, probably back home to her family. I know she resented being brought here." Mother Gabriel shook her head in dismay. The white wings on either side of her headdress bobbed up and down. "I have developed a special fondness for Julia." To her surprise, Susan detected a slight twitch at the corner of Mother Gabriel's mouth and an uncustomary moistness in her eyes. "Did Julia say anything to any of you girls about her plans?" she asked. Again, the girls looked at each other, then shook their heads.

"It wasn't just the news that upset her," Susan said after a moment. She hung her head. "I told her that her father had been taken to a labor camp and she was very upset over that."

"Ah," Mother Gabriel nodded with understanding.

"Yes, Julia is fearless," she continued, "and concern for her family was probably all she needed as a final incentive to leave." Mother Gabriel sighed and folded her hands in her lap. "Let's hope she made it back safely. Unfortunately, for the sake of everyone's safety here, we can't do much to find her or to get her back. But," she added in a hushed tone, "Sister Ibi told me that one of the nun's gowns had disappeared from the laundry room. She found an empty hanger dangling in the midst of a row of freshly pressed habits. And right after Mass, Sister Teresa asked me if I had any more of those Swedish documents. She seems to have misplaced hers. I have a feeling," she nodded knowingly, "that our

Julia is not only headstrong, but clever as well. She picked the perfect disguise to keep herself from getting into trouble with the Nazis."

Susan was relieved at the thought that Julia might get back to her mother safely. Maybe she would convince Mama to get her and Vera back during this difficult time. But no, it was foolish to think that. Mama wanted her and Vera to be here. The best thing Susan could do was stick to her promise to look after Vera. Still, she wished she had just a bit of Julia's courage.

At recreation time, not being in the mood to join the other girls, Susan walked alone in the garden. Lost in thought, she weaved in and out between the barren flower beds.

"I love this time of early spring, just before everything starts to grow and blossom," Sister Agnes's voice startled Susan. She had almost bumped right into the nun who was bent down, examining an empty plot of brown earth. Sister Agnes smiled up at her. "I like the anticipation, knowing that even though we can't actually see anything yet, there is a lot of work going on underground." She skimmed her hands lovingly over the surface of the moist, brown soil. "The roots thawing out, gaining strength," she said softly, "the new shoots starting to grow beneath the surface. Any day now the first green tips will poke their way through." She stood up and turned to face Susan.

"I know Julia's disappearance is very disturbing, especially for you," she said, suddenly changing the subject. "She is your cousin and you both have a great sense of responsibility toward your families – and that is very good." She paused, searching for the right words. Her forehead wrinkled beneath the white headgear. Not a single strand of hair showed, and Susan realized that she had no idea what color Sister Agnes's hair was. Perhaps brown, like her eyebrows.

"Except that I'm not brave, like Julia," Susan blurted out. She turned and started walking back along the path. Sister Agnes fell in step beside her.

"Running away, like Julia did, isn't necessarily the only way to be brave," she said. She placed her arm gently around Susan's shoulders. "Staying here and contributing to our community takes courage, too. It's just a different kind of courage."

"It sure doesn't feel like there's anything courageous about staying here," Susan hung her head. "We're just hiding, doing nothing."

"Doing nothing?" Sister Agnes stopped and turned her around so that they were facing each other. "Do you think that your work in the kitchen and laundry room and your help with the younger children is doing nothing? In order for this place to function smoothly, we need everybody to help out. You are very capable, one of the girls whom we can count on to do a job well. And soon there will be the garden as well." She waved her arms around the expanse of the convent grounds. "Doing all these things might seem ordinary and trivial, but think of all the people who would suffer if they didn't get done. Doing these ordinary tasks is as heroic as going off to fight in the war. It all depends on what you are meant to do."

Susan looked down, feeling better, but at the same time embarrassed by Sister Agnes's praise.

"What about Julia?" she asked. "Do you think she was meant to leave?"

"I don't know," Sister Agnes shook her head. "All I know is that we must pray for her safety. And we must trust that somehow everything will work out," she added. "That is what faith is about."

Susan shook her head, "It's so hard to have faith," she said.

"Yes," Sister Agnes agreed, her voice almost a whisper, "sometimes it can be very difficult."

Chapter 16

Passover in the Convent

April 1944

With the worsening conditions for Jews, more girls arrived at the convent every day. Sisters Agnes set up another room with beds. Two more long tables were added in the dining room. The sessions of work in the laundry room and kitchen grew longer and school time shorter. The older girls took turns playing games or reading with the younger ones.

Susan gave up trying to keep track of the names of all the new girls, but she enjoyed having more girls her own age around. She realized how isolated she had become in the weeks before she came to the convent. There was always something to do and, these days, always someone to do it with.

It became more difficult to concentrate on regular school lessons.

Math and poetry seemed unimportant in a world filled with tanks and soldiers. Sister Agnes allowed the girls to set up a separate class with a bulletin board of newspaper clippings and a large map on which they could follow the progress of the war. In this room they could talk freely about world events and ask questions that the nuns did their best to answer. Susan joined Ester and some of the older girls in studying Jewish history. Mostly, they taught themselves, each researching a time in history and presenting it to the group. Sister Teresa, whose expertise was history, answered their more difficult questions.

In the midst of all this activity, Susan would hear the rumble of a tank in the street, or glimpse a uniformed soldier walking past the gates.

With the arrival of April, the nuns began preparations for their most solemn celebration of the year, Easter. Until now, Susan had not realized that this holiday was linked to the Jewish holiday of Passover.

"Did you know," she asked Ester during one of their study sessions, "that next Thursday, just before Easter, is the day the Catholics celebrate Jesus' last supper? They call it Holy Thursday. Sister Agnes told me that the Last Supper was actually a seder, the ritual Passover meal. The nuns here have a special meal that night, too, trying to make it a bit like Jesus' Passover meal."

"But do they know about matzoh?" asked Anna. "I mean, do they know what the Passover seder is like?"

"Jesus was a Jew, so he would have done something similar to what we do." Susan took a big breath, excited with her new plan. "I asked Sister Agnes if we could have a Passover seder. And she discussed it with Mother Gabriel who said we could try it. She wants us to do it together with one of the nuns, Sister Teresa, explaining about Jesus and some things he added or changed in the Jewish rituals.

She paused and looked imploringly at Ester. "Do you think we could do a seder with you leading it? I know it's usually led by the man of the house, but here you would be the best one to do it."

Ester hesitated. "It's not as simple as lighting the candles. There is a special order to the seder. And there are symbolic things we need, like the matzoh."

"We'll do the best we can from our memory. And we could figure out a way to make unleavened bread without flour or yeast. I'm sure Sister Magda would agree to bake and cook whatever we tell her, as long as she can get the ingredients," replied Susan. "Between all of us, we can surely explain the main rituals and recite the Passover story. Those are the most important parts."

"You certainly have an answer for everything," Ester laughed. "Well, it would be good practice for me to organize a seder with you."

"And the others can help, too. We all remember how we celebrated our holidays at home, right?" Susan looked at the other girls sitting around the table. They all nodded in agreement.

Over the next couple of days, the girls helped plan the ritual part of the seder as well as the meal. Susan noticed with amusement that Ester was often reading the New Testament, while Sister Teresa was poring over the story of Exodus in the Old Testament, the Jewish Bible. Then their heads would bend together in animated conversation.

She and Anna helped Sister Magda prepare the foods for the seder plate. They needed some parsley, a roasted egg, bitter greens, and a roasted shank bone. They also had to make *charoses*, a mixture of nuts, sweet wine, and raisins that symbolized the bricks Jewish slaves used when they were forced to build the Egyptian pyramids. And the salt water, for the "tears" of the slaves, was easy to prepare.

On the first night of Passover, an excited group gathered in the dining room. Both the nuns and the girls seemed equally curious to learn about each other's customs.

Susan sat on the dining-room bench next to Vera, holding her hand. On this holiday, in particular, Jewish families came together. Susan remembered their Passover celebrations at home with the whole family and some invited friends around the large dining room table with its starched white linens and silver candlesticks. The flickering holiday candles would shine on Papa's face as he read from the Haggadah, the special book of readings for Passover. Her stomach always grumbled with hunger during the long ceremony of the seder, as the tantalizing smells of chicken soup with matzoh balls drifted in from the kitchen.

At the convent, they had arranged the tables in a large square around the dining room. Ester sat with Sister Teresa at a table in the center. On the white cloth in front of them was a makeshift seder plate, a stack of their homemade "unleavened bread," and a bottle of red wine.

"Is Ester pretending to be Papa?" Vera whispered to Susan.

"Yes," Susan whispered back, "but we must be quiet now." A hush fell over the room. Ester lifted her head, her long hair covered with a shawl and began.

"*Barukh ata adonai eloheinu melekh ha-olam....*"

When Ester finished the first blessing, Sister Teresa began.

"Bless us, oh Lord, and these Thy gifts…"

Susan watched mesmerized as the celebration continued, a solemn duet, with Ester leading the seder, then pausing as Sister Teresa added a Christian prayer or a further explanation of the rituals.

Taking turns, Ester and Sister Teresa recounted the Exodus story – the story of how the Jewish people were led by Moses from a life of slavery in Egypt to freedom in the Promised Land. This time, the story of Moses had new meaning for Susan. Moses, too, had been hidden as a child, at a time when his people were persecuted.

Ester and Sister Teresa each held up a piece of the unleavened bread.

"This is the bread of affliction, which our ancestors ate in the land of Egypt. All who are hungry, let them come and eat…" Ester recited.

"This is my body, which will be given up for you…" Sister Teresa followed.

"Blessed are you, lord our God, ruler of the universe, creator of the fruit of the vine."

"This is my blood of the new covenant."

At first Susan found Sister Teresa's interjections awkward, but as the ritual progressed, she found that she understood better what the priest did during morning Mass. He also held up the bread and wine and blessed them. She had thought that this celebration would show the nuns how Jews did things differently. Yet now she saw how their customs were related. This celebration had brought them all closer together.

When the food was at long last brought out of the kitchen, it was indeed a feast.

"There are no matzoh balls," Vera complained when she looked down into the steaming bowl of soup in front of her.

"From where would Sister Magda get matzoh balls?" asked Susan. "You should be glad she made such good soup for us." Silently to herself she added, *I'm sure Mama isn't having any either. She might not even be having any soup at all.*

For a brief time, the girls had been so busy with the seder, they almost forgot about the Nazis.

Chapter 17

The Vegetable Garden

Daily news trickled into the convent from the surrounding city. Each evening Mother Gabriel read the main headlines from the newspaper and told them what was happening in their area. To this, the nuns who worked in the city added their stories. Mother Gabriel told the girls about the arrest of hundreds of prominent Hungarian Jews, the creation of the ghetto, and the transfer of all property and valuables owned by Jews into Nazi hands. Toward the end of the April, they heard that most public schools in the city were locked and boarded up. Some of the schools became "designated" Jewish buildings, outside the ghetto walls, but marked with a large yellow star. Numerous families were crowded together in these buildings – after their own homes had been taken away.

New Jewish girls continued to arrive every day with their own stories of the ill treatment their families had suffered. Several of them were very young, barely four or five years old. Vera could no longer boast of being the youngest. Susan estimated that there must now be close to one hundred Jewish girls in the convent. Although the German Nazis and the Hungarian Arrow Cross Party left them alone, Mother Gabriel still insisted that the girls play away from the road and fences where they could be seen.

With all the extra girls, there were many more chores to do. Yet, as she worked in the kitchen or laundry room or read to the younger girls, Susan felt increasingly content. She knew she was a good worker and that her help was needed. And though she didn't spend much time directly with Vera, she knew that everything she did contributed to her little sister's well being. *I am taking good care of Vera, Mama,* she whispered confidently each night before closing her eyes.

Not all chores felt like work to Susan. Tending the garden became one of her favorite pastimes. Each day when they went outside for their fresh air and exercise, Sister Agnes would ask a few of the girls to help her loosen the soil around the new shoots, pull out unwanted weeds, or replant those flowers that had spread too far or were doing poorly in their current location. Susan always volunteered to work in the garden. She liked digging with her fingers in the moist brown soil, gently feeling for the roots with her fingertips. She was always careful not to damage them or expose them to the drying air for too long. She preferred working among the flowers to throwing balls or skipping with the younger girls.

One day in early May, as she sat back to admire the contrast between the dark, freshly turned soil and the delicate light green stems rising out of it, Sister Agnes joined her.

"I could tell from the beginning that you were a natural at this," she said with satisfaction as she looked at Susan's dirt encrusted fingers. "You have a gift for helping things grow. Not too many people like to dig with their bare hands. Most prefer to wear gloves and use those small trowels."

"Oh, I start with the trowel," Susan explained self-consciously, "but when I get close to the roots it's too dangerous. I have to use my fingers to feel my way."

"Yes, exactly. That's what I meant," nodded Sister Agnes. She paused for a minute looking thoughtfully at the newly formed rosebuds on the bush beside Susan. "Come with me," she said with a secretive glint in her eyes. "There's another garden back here that you might like to help with as well." She led Susan along several meandering paths, between beds of flowers and towering trees, always ascending the steep hillside. Above their heads, the chestnuts were in full blossom and their tall spray of white and pink flowers pointed toward the blue sky like hundreds of ornate candelabras.

Sister Agnes stopped at a strip of level ground running along almost the entire length of the fence at the rear of the garden. The barren earth here looked freshly turned.

"This is our vegetable garden," announced Sister Agnes proudly. "I convinced Mother Gabriel to let me try to grow a few vegetables here.

That first year it was only a few square meters, purely an experiment. But as you can see, it is a fairly substantial garden now." She waved her arm proudly over the expanse of ground in front of them. "It is very satisfying to eat food we have grown ourselves. We grow enough now that Sister Magda can actually use some of the vegetables in her meal preparation. And see, over there," she said pointing to their right, "there are a few cherry, pear, and apple trees." Susan turned and breathed in the sweet fragrance of the fruit blossoms.

"Would you like to help?" Sister Agnes asked. "I've already planted potatoes, carrots, and onions over there. Today I was going to put in the tomatoes and green peppers." Without waiting for a reply, she turned and walked to a small shed hidden behind the fruit trees. At first, Susan could see nothing of the gloomy interior. It was her nose that told her of the presence of musty tools, damp earth, and a faint hint of green, living things. Mint? Perhaps camomile? As her eyes adjusted she saw that Sister Agnes was already standing on a short wooden ladder, handing down clay pots of small green plants from a shelf against the back wall. Susan hurried over and carefully took them from her, one by one. With her foot, Sister Agnes indicated a weathered wheelbarrow at her side. Susan placed the pots inside.

"I planted these seeds in here a few weeks ago. Now they will grow better in the garden with a bit of a head start." For the next hour, Sister Agnes and Susan worked busily side by side planting the seedlings and pulling out weeds. By the end, Susan's knees and back were sore and her tunic clung damply to her back. She wondered if the creases of her knuckles would ever be clean again. Sister Agnes's headdress had tilted sideways on her head and streaks of dirt ran across her forehead and down her cheeks. But it was satisfying work.

Throughout the spring and summer, Susan helped in the vegetable garden every day. It soon became her favorite job. Once everything was planted, the plots had to be weeded and watered regularly. The water had to be hauled in buckets from the well close behind the convent building. Sometimes Ester, Anna, or some of the other nuns joined her. But Susan was the only one Sister Agnes trusted to work there by herself.

Each day, Susan's eyes searched the rich brown soil for a sign that their efforts were worthwhile. She knew that there, beneath the earth, hidden from her eyes, wonderful work was going on. Slowly, one by one, the potatoes, the carrots, the beans poked their new green shoots above the surface. The tomato vines climbed along the back fence, the fruit trees dropped their blossoms and small round fruits soon took their place.

"I can't wait to see the tomatoes actually growing and turning red!" she exclaimed one day. But then she quickly clamped her hand over her mouth as she realized what she had just said. It would be fall before the vegetables and fruits ripened. Did she really hope to stay here that long? Feeling guilty and confused, she shrugged the thought away.

She looked toward the city below them, now completely hidden from view by the lush green foliage of the trees. Working in the garden, occupied with bringing things to life, it was easy to forget that just on the other side of the fence, death and suffering reigned. With all her activities, she had grown so involved in her new life that at times she forgot to think of her parents and little brother. It was only at night, just before she drifted off to sleep, that her thoughts always turned toward her family.

Then, on a hot, windless night at the end of August, when every leaf in the orchard stood still and only the buzz of insects disturbed the air, Susan received some unexpected news from home.

Chapter 18

News from Home

August 1944

Julia arrived at the convent wearing the stained and wrinkled nun's habit that had disappeared from the laundry room. Mother Gabriel met her at the door and after the exchange of a few hushed sentences ushered her off to the nun's private infirmary. Susan found her late the next morning, sitting motionless by the old classroom window, gazing out at the younger girls playing ball outside.

"Julia!" Susan exclaimed. "I didn't know you were back. When did you get here? What happened? How is your family? Did you see my mother?" her words tumbled out as she hurried over to her cousin. She could tell immediately that Julia had changed. Though her back was straight, her shoulders were slumped, her arms wrapped tightly around herself as if in protection from the outside world.

"Susan," Julia turned a tear-stained face to her, and Susan saw that her old defiance had been replaced by sorrow. "I came back last night and Mother Gabriel insisted I sleep in the infirmary and get a good rest before talking with you." She pressed her lips together and her brow furrowed. Slowly, letting out a deep sigh, she regarded Susan.

"I'm sorry," Julia spoke in a measured tone as if carefully considering each word uttered. "I don't really see any way around telling you the truth. Mother Gabriel says that facing the truth is best. Even when it's hard."

Susan reached a hand up to her chest to steady the violent beating of her heart. *What had happened?*

"There was nothing I could do." Julia looked down, her voice trembling. "They took your mother and Tomas. They took my Mama too, but they put them on different trucks."

"Who took Mama and Tomas away?" asked Susan.

"The Nazis. And it's not just the Germans. Many of them are Hungarian soldiers, members of the Arrow Cross. They are Nazis too, and they work together. Every day they come into the ghetto and round up Jewish people. They force them into trucks or just march them out. No one knows who will be next."

Julia took a deep breath to steady her voice. "I went back," Julia continued, "because I thought I could help." She shook her head again as if trying to shake the images from her mind. "At first, I thought I could get back with the underground resistance group that I was working with before coming here. But they are all gone, escaped, or captured. Inside the ghetto, there is so little anyone can do – except hide. Susan, we are so fortunate to be here. Our parents were right to send us here when they did."

Susan was surprised to hear this from Julia. She knelt down by her cousin's chair. She had to know more. "When did they take Mama and Tomas?"

"It was the day before yesterday." Julia wiped her eyes. "They were living together, your mother and mine, in the building above the jeweler's shop near the school. It's all part of the Jewish ghetto now."

She shook her head. "It's a horrible place, the ghetto. An area of the city is all walled in with guards at the gates. Inside, everyone is crowded together with very few belongings. Mama said they were only allowed to grab a couple of things from their homes before they were forced to move. And there is so little food. My mother said that your Aunt Isi had somehow arranged with your mother to throw a small sack of food over the ghetto walls at a certain time and place every few days. We survived with her help for a long time. But a couple of weeks ago, the sacks stopped dropping over the wall. We haven't heard from your Aunt Isi since. We were so hungry. Poor Tomas was always crying."

There was a long, heavy silence. Finally Susan swallowed and asked in a fearful whisper, "Where were they taken?"

Julia looked down at her hands now resting in her lap.

"I don't know. I don't think anyone knows," she replied with exasperation. "There are only horrible rumors about the deportations." She paused, took a big breath and, seeming to come to a decision, looked up at Susan.

"You may as well know all of it. Some people say that the Jews are taken to labor camps like the ones where our fathers were taken. They get very little food, but still have to do heavy work for long hours to help the Germans build war equipment. Other people say that the Germans now have death camps, where children and elderly people are taken to be killed. Sometimes women with babies are taken there."

Susan clasped her hand to her mouth. What Julia was saying was too horrible to believe.

Julia continued, "There have been some witnesses. A man from Poland escaped from one of those camps. He fled to Budapest last year when it was still safe. In the ghetto, he talked about a place called Auschwitz, where there are gas chambers for killing people. He had seen it with his own eyes."

Susan now desperately needed to know about her own family. "Did you see my mother and Tomas get taken away?"

Julia looked out the window, hesitating. "Every day we heard the trucks coming down the street." Her voice was slow and even again, as if she were watching the scene replayed outside the window. "I didn't think they would be coming for us. There were about ten other people living in that tiny apartment with us. Those trucks came every day. I thought they would continue to pass us by.

"But my mother was more cautious. She showed me where to hide – just in case. Down below, in the store, there was a large empty display cabinet. Under the bottom shelf was a storage area. On the day when the trucks came for them, she pushed me in there and closed the cabinet behind me."

Julia bit her bottom lip, and the tears trickled down her cheeks. "When I pushed up with my head, the bottom shelf lifted slightly and I could see through a small space of glass. The Nazis had a list. They read the names off, checked the papers, and shoved the people out the door toward the trucks. They had the names of both of our mothers. My name was not on their list, so they weren't looking for me.

"At first our mothers were led toward the same truck. But, before they got in, one of the men tried to take Tomas from your mother. She wouldn't let him go." Julia sighed. She looked down at her hands, white and clenched in her lap. "They dragged her toward another truck. She got on with Tomas and then they left." Julia let out a long breath, deflated.

"Didn't anybody say where they were going?" Susan asked again. "Which camp? Didn't the soldiers say?"

Julia shook her head slowly. "That's all I know," she finally answered before she continued with her story. "Before my mother shoved me into the cabinet, she told me to come back here to the nuns. She said that the only thing that would make all this bearable for her was to know that I was safe. So I stayed in the cabinet. I escaped that night. I didn't see anybody. I couldn't stay there after that. I hadn't helped. I didn't even try to stop the soldiers."

Susan had no words of comfort for Julia. She was so upset herself.

"What about *my* Mama? Did *she* say anything?" Did she have any message for me?" Susan asked desperately.

Julia refocused her eyes on Susan. "Yes, she did. I almost forgot. She ran over to me, just as my mother was shutting the cabinet door. She put her hand on the door and stopped it from shutting. I thought she was going to hand Tomas to me. But she wouldn't let go of him. She was afraid he would cry out and then we would both be discovered. She said to tell you that she loved you and that you are always to take care of Vera. And she gave me this." Julia's right hand fumbled in the pocket of her dress. She pressed a dog-eared piece of paper into Susan's hand.

Susan turned it over. It was a photograph of Mama, Papa, Tomas, Vera, and herself, each one smiling.

Chapter 19

A Conversation
with Sister Agnes

Photograph in hand, Susan ran from the room. She ran down the long hall, down the steps and out the back door, up the hill to her refuge – the vegetable garden. She passed a blur of bodies and faces.

She didn't think about where she was going. She just knew she needed to get far away from Julia's words. She had to calm herself and wipe out the horrible images that swirled in her head. When she finally focused on the outside world again, Susan was kneeling in the garden, looking down at the rows of flourishing peppers, cucumbers, and tomato plants.

She looked from the lush garden to the photograph still clutched in her hand. It was all a lie. The garden's promise of peace and plenty was as false as the promise of a happy family portrayed in the picture. She stuck the photo in her pocket. Then, with her right hand she reached out, plucked a large green tomato and threw it hard. Tomato pulp splattered on the brown fence behind. It brought her little satisfaction. She reached for another tomato.

"You've spoken with Julia." Sister Agnes's voice halted the swing of Susan's arm. Her arm went limp. She let the tomato drop. She did not turn to look at Sister Agnes.

"I'm sorry about your mother and little brother." Sister Agnes looked down at the tomato and up at the fence. "I know how difficult this must be – to know that people you love are suffering and that there is nothing you can do."

"You don't know. You can't know," Susan said angrily, without turning to look at the nun. "You don't have a family. You just hide away here. You don't really care."

The silence following her outburst was so long that for a minute Susan wondered if Sister Agnes had heard her.

The nun sank down on her knees next to Susan. "I do have a family," she said quietly. "I have a mother and a father and a brother. They all live in the city, near the base of Gellert Mountain."

Susan was surprised to hear Sister Agnes's words. She had never thought about the lives of any of the nuns outside the convent. Yet they must all have a past and a family. "Why did you come here?" she asked, suddenly curious. "Why did you decide to become a nun?"

Again there was a long silence. Susan glanced up at Sister Agnes who had a faraway look in her eyes.

"I guess my decision started when I was a little girl," she began, "probably just a couple of years older than Vera. I was about eight when I first came here with my mother. We were dropping off some used clothes for the nuns to give to the orphans in their care. The Sisters had been kind to us when my father was ill and couldn't work for several months. They brought us food each day. We were very grateful.

"After my father's illness, my mother began coming to the church here to show our support for the kind Sisters."

As Sister Agnes talked, Susan's body relaxed. The nun's voice was soft and soothing. A gentle breeze began to blow around them, a welcome change from the oppressive heat of the past few days. Susan lost herself in the story, distracted from her own sorrow.

"I remember stepping inside the cool, solemn silence of the church for the first time," Sister Agnes went on. "It was easy to pray here and to be thankful for the beauty of the world."

"After Mass, we waited in the convent's large foyer for the Mother Superior to come and receive our gifts in person. She offered to show us the convent and their work. I grasped her hand readily and followed her as she led me along, opening doors to the dormitories and study halls filled with girls of all ages, some playing, some studying. Always nuns moved quietly among them, helping, sometimes teaching or joining in light-hearted laughter."

Susan tried to picture a young Sister Agnes, walking hand in hand beside the Mother Superior.

"As we walked, the Mother Superior explained to me about their order. Of course, I didn't understand everything. But the caring atmosphere made a deep impression on me. At the end of the tour, the Mother Superior asked me what I thought of their home. Without hesitation, I said that I would like to live there when I grew up. Unlike my mother, who laughed at my childish enthusiasm, the Mother Superior took me seriously. She invited us to visit anytime.

"Of course, it was several years before I was old enough to come here unattended by my mother. But when I could, I came almost every weekend and sometimes, if I could sneak away from home, even during the week after school. I loved helping with the younger girls, to see the light in their eyes when they understood something I had explained. And all the nuns always made me feel so welcome. I felt needed – like I was the best I could be whenever I was here." Sister Agnes's whole face seemed to glow with this memory

Susan regarded her thoughtfully. It was true. By helping with all the work, taking care of others, Susan, too, felt needed. There were even times when she had caught herself thinking: *How would they ever get along without me?*

Sister Agnes continued, "As soon as I turned eighteen, I asked if I could become part of the convent community."

"Did you never think of getting married?" asked Susan. "Weren't you ever in love?" Sister Agnes laughed lightly and thought for a moment as if wanting to make sure she answered truthfully.

"I was friends with several young men," she replied, "but never in a romantic way. Though it was fun to do things with them, my feelings for them were never as strong as my love for God. The only man who ever became a close friend was Viktor, who first arranged for Anna and Panni to come here. But he understood right from the beginning about my desire to join the convent.

"Also, if I was to marry and have a family," Sister Agnes added, "I couldn't dedicate myself fully to serving others, as I do here." Susan thought of Aunt Isi. She, too, seemed to be dedicated to helping others.

"These days," Sister Agnes was speaking again, but almost inaudibly, as if she were talking to herself, "I think that my whole life has been a preparation for this time, for what we are doing now, hiding all of you girls. I wouldn't give this opportunity up for anything. It is how I can help, in a very small way, to make the world right again." She looked at Susan and wrapped her arms around her.

"I have never regretted my decision," she said with a nod of determination. They sat there for a while. Slowly, the truth of Julia's news once again haunted Susan.

"So what can I to do now that my family has been sent away?" she asked Sister Agnes quietly.

"I am very sorry about your mother and little brother," Sister Agnes said. "Though there is nothing you can do to help them, you can take comfort in the knowledge that your and Vera's safe presence here may give your mother some joy and hope. Make the most of it. You can strive to be the best you can be. That way, when she sees you again, your mother will be proud of who you have become."

She paused and reached for the green tomato that still lay on the ground between them. Absentmindedly, she rolled it over and handed it to Susan.

"There's no point in wasting this," said Sister Agnes. "Though it is no longer on the vine, if we place it in the warmth of the sun, it will ripen."

Chapter 20

Harvest

September 1944

The sweltering summer days melted from August into September. It seemed to Susan that the world had been at war forever. The rumble of distant fighting drifted over the convent walls and frequently the evening horizon was aglow with the fiery orange haze of battle.

"The Allied troops – our friends from Britain, America, and Russia – are beginning to win the war," Mother Gabriel told them. "They are attacking the Nazi invaders across Europe. The Nazis are retreating from France, Belgium, and other Eastern European countries."

She explained to the girls that this might mean harder times for the people of Hungary. "The Nazis are putting more pressure on our country since it is among the few where they are still in control. And they will try to protect their main strongholds, like the one here on

Mount Gellert." She paused and then added, "Even our peaceful existence here at the convent could be endangered. We may face more difficult times together before the war is over."

While Mother Gabriel's premonitions disturbed Susan, the constant work to be done, especially in the garden, demanded more immediate attention. With the onset of autumn, the work in the vegetable garden had shifted to harvesting. By late September, they had picked most of the fruits and vegetables. Though the quantities they grew were not large, the fresh beans, tomatoes, and green peppers were a welcome addition to their meals. There was an ever-increasing shortage of food in the city. Each time Sister Magda made stew, it seemed a bit more watery. The slices of bread grew thinner and thinner. All the girls were eager to help in the kitchen now and take advantage of the extra nibbles of food they were allowed to have there.

Susan felt a moment of panic on the last day in early October when she and Sister Agnes knelt in front of the neat rows of potato, carrot, and onion plants. Empty baskets stood at their side in readiness to be filled with this final harvest. Perhaps, when she reached down into the dark soil, her fingers would find nothing. All summer these three vegetables had caused her the greatest concern. There was plenty of green growth above ground, but what if there was nothing below? She had asked Sister Agnes several times if she could dig up just one of the plants, but Sister Agnes said they would just have to trust and wait.

On the day of their harvesting, Susan reached out and gently eased her hand around the roots of the first plant. Her fingers felt out one, then two, then three large, firm, round potatoes. She triumphantly yanked the entire plant out of the soil, revealing six potatoes. Both she and Sister Agnes clapped their hands and hugged one another. Next, Sister Agnes pulled out a cluster of long orange carrots.

"Perhaps Sister Magda will let us have a bit of a feast tonight instead of the careful way she rations food these days," she said laughing.

Sister Magda was more than happy to add the fresh produce of the garden to the soup she was making. For the first time in weeks they all walked away full and satisfied from the dining room. A light-hearted evening of games and stories followed. Looking back, a few weeks later, Susan was glad that they had had that final day of celebration before events took a dramatic turn for the worse.

The Nazis fortified Gellert Mountain.

On October 15, the dreaded Arrow Cross Party replaced the temporary government that had been established by the invading Nazis. Like the Nazis, the Hungarian Arrow Cross was a political party that promoted the persecution of Jews. Within days, this new government began murdering Jews by the hundreds. Thousands more were deported.

Battles raged in the towns and villages of Hungary as the Russian army attacked from the air, seeking to take control. The Nazi and Arrow Cross armies fought equally hard to drive them back. Yet slowly, the Russians advanced upon the city of Budapest.

The Nazi battalions above the convent, and on the surrounding mountaintops, were in a constant state of alert, their canons aimed in readiness at the sky. For the people of the city, the hardships worsened with each passing day. In the relative safety of the convent, Susan and the other girls followed the progress of events with increasing apprehension.

And as Mother Gabriel had expected, by early November, the Convent of the Sisters of Charity was caught in the middle of a battle.

Part Three
Battleground

Chapter 21

Night of Explosions

November 2, 1944

Susan lay on her back and gazed out at the thin crescent moon that peeked in through the window facing her bed. She could hear the receding footsteps of Sister Agnes and her assistant as they finished making their nightly rounds. She heard the gentle click of the latch as the dormitory door shut behind them. She closed her eyes.

Suddenly, a fiery orange glow transformed the slumber-laden room. Susan bolted upright, swung her legs over the side of the bed and ran to the window.

"What is that?" she exclaimed, her hand clutching the window frame. "Is the building on fire?"

"It's in the sky. Look there," Anna, who had come up behind her, pointed. From where they stood, they could see a bright orange light, slowly descending in the rectangle of sky, shedding an unnatural blush upon the whole city. Other girls crowded around them. As they watched, another sinking light appeared. Within seconds, the roar of a fleet of planes filled their ears, followed by loud explosions. The windows shook and rumbled.

The dormitory door flew open and Sister Agnes rushed back in.

"Girls, the city is under attack!" Though her eyes darted here and there to make sure they were all right, her voice was steady. "Please stay calm. We must – "

"Every one, please go to the dining room at once!" Mother Gabriel's imperial command interrupted from the hallway.

Questions flew from several directions.

"What's happening?"

"Are we being bombed?"

"Yes, we are being bombed," Mother Gabriel explained. "Those are Russian planes above us. They are trying to destroy the Nazi army bases in the city, like the one on the mountaintop above us. If the Russians are victorious, the Nazis will retreat from here and we will be free. In the meantime, we need to look out for our own safety."

Then she continued with instructions to the girls. "Stay calm and follow Sister Agnes to the dining room. I will alert the girls in the other rooms."

The girls followed Sister Agnes down the dark corridor. "We mustn't turn on the lights," Sister Agnes said curtly as Anna reached for the light switch. "Lights will make us more visible, a target for the bombs. We must be especially cautious because the Nazi headquarters is next door to us."

It was hard to stay calm. Susan's heart pounded violently as she felt her way down the stairs. But there was no time to indulge in her fears. The roar of planes and explosions, now mingled with the panicked cry of little girls, drove from her mind everything except getting to safety. Thankfully, the glow from the flares kept the hallway and stairwell from being pitch black. It seemed an eternity before they were all safely huddled together in the dark dining room. There, Susan found Vera, who gratefully snuggled into her arms.

The eerie, orange light faded from the windows and they sat in darkness listening to the steady roar of planes, punctuated by the frequent explosions. The ground beneath them trembled and the roar of the planes seemed to penetrate Susan's bones. Everyone jumped and several girls screamed when a window shattered, blowing in a sudden draft of cold air.

"Are they firing right at us?" someone asked.

"Of course not," Mother Gabriel's steady voice rose above the noise. "That window broke because the ground around us is vibrating from the force of those guns. Next time we will find a safer place to hide."

Next time? Susan sat up in fear. *Will there be a next time?* She had hoped the Russians would defeat the Nazis tonight. Gently rocking Vera back and forth, she listened to the voices of the nuns around her. It was clear to them that the events of this night would repeat themselves for many more days. It would take several battles before the Nazi soldiers would retreat from their place on the mountain. She wrapped her arms tighter around her little sister.

Chapter 22

The Crypt

Susan trudged mechanically along the stone path to the predawn Mass. Her head felt groggier than usual, and several times she stumbled against Anna in front of her. The garden, bathed in dew, sparkled peacefully. The chaos of the previous night seemed like a bad dream. There was no sign yet that anything unusual had happened. Except that this time Vera walked beside her, holding her hand. She was too fearful now to stay behind alone.

Right after breakfast, Mother Gabriel requested a special meeting with the girls. At once everyone became alert. Perhaps the Russians had made a quick victory after all and they could all go home!

"My children," Mother Gabriel began when they were finally all quiet. "I am sorry for the confusion last night. We should have anticipated that eventually Budapest would be attacked, and we should have been better prepared. I heard on the radio this morning…" A couple of gasps were audible, and several of the girls looked at each other with raised eyebrows. Mother Gabriel listened to the radio? They didn't even know the convent had one.

Mother Gabriel didn't miss their surprise. "Yes, I have a radio," she said looking around at them with a twinkle in her eye. "Mr. Majori brought it to me after the invasion. He said I might need it for up-to-date news. After last night's attack, it was important to know what was happening."

All the girls held their breath as they waited to hear what she had to say. The Russians had reached the eastern border of Budapest, and they were attempting to take control of the city. The Nazis were aggressively fighting back. Until yesterday, the battles had been on the ground, but last night, Russian planes flew over Budapest, bombing the Nazi artillery bases.

"The orange flares you saw," she explained, "are dropped to light their way. The Nazis have imposed a curfew. Everyone has to be off the streets by seven o'clock."

Clearly, Mother Gabriel was not about to announce a triumphant victory. Susan sighed and settled back in her chair. She hoped they would be allowed to go back to bed for a while. However, as she listened to Mother Gabriel's words, it was evident that was not the case. Instead, she told them that from now on, a loud siren would sound from various parts of the city so that people could hide below ground before an attack.

"I spoke with some of the other Sisters," explained Mother Gabriel, "and we decided that the safest place for us to hide is in the crypt beneath the church."

A crypt? Beneath the church? Susan exchanged glances with Anna and Julia who sat on either side of her. The rest of the girls looked equally surprised.

"What's a crypt?" Susan asked.

"It is a large stone room underground, beneath the church. It holds the caskets of all the Mother Superiors of this convent who have died. There are no windows in the crypt so we won't need to worry about broken glass and cold air blowing in. Also, there is less risk because the Russians are unlikely to bomb a church."

Hiding in a room with caskets! Again, everyone was talking at once. The tinkling of Mother Gabriel's bell silenced them.

Anna spoke for them all when she asked, "Are we really going to be in the same room with dead bodies?"

Mother Gabriel smiled. "Those 'dead' bodies are in caskets which are located at the opposite end of the room from where we will be. It is a very large room, almost the entire length of the church. I will arrange for some kind of a barrier to separate us from the caskets. It will be more respectful."

For the first time, it occurred to Susan how old and tired the Mother Superior looked. Her normally straight back was bent and her shoulders stooped. The once mirthful lines around her eyes and mouth had transformed into worry lines.

"Our biggest problem is getting to the church," she said after a pause. "We will have to be well-prepared to run there at a moment's notice. The alarm might sound in the middle of the night when it is cold and raining, or snowing if this continues long enough."

She then carefully outlined the procedure for the girls and insisted there be a few practice runs so they would be prepared.

"We will use the back exit through the kitchen and take the path of the Stations of the Cross to get to the church. The path looks like it ends near the bushes at the back of the church. But behind the bushes is a small wooden door, which is the only outside entrance to the crypt." They all gasped. A secret door!

"I chose this path because it is well-concealed from the road and other buildings. No one will see us coming or going. The other entrance to the crypt, from inside the sacristy – the room behind the altar where the priest's vestments and sacred vessels are kept – will be immediately boarded up and painted over," she raised her eyebrows. "No one will be able to tell that it was ever an entrance to the crypt."

"But will we be safe there?" one of the girls asked.

"It is the best we can do," Mother Gabriel said. "We will prepare the room with extra blankets, candles, drinking water, and food."

"What if the Nazis find the back door and come in? We will have no way of getting out," Anna asked, terrified at the thought.

"They have no reason to come snooping around the church," Mother Gabriel said firmly. "But if they do, I doubt they would notice the door behind all those bushes. I'm sure you have walked right by it many times. Has anyone noticed it before?" They looked at one another and shook their heads. Nobody was aware of a door behind the bushes.

"The Nazis would be more likely to examine doors from the inside, if they ever did enter the church." Mother Gabriel reassured them. "And remember, we are still under Swedish protection. The Nazis have no right to visit our grounds. Let's just hope the war will be over soon and that the Russians are successful in getting rid of the Nazis." The girls nodded their heads in agreement.

"Let's get ready for our first practice session now. This one you can prepare for. The sirens will come unannounced. Remember, there are soldiers all around us. We don't want to do anything to attract their attention." With a slight nod of encouragement, Mother Gabriel left the room.

Chapter 23

In the Shelter

The penetrating blast of sound began as a low wail and mounted rapidly in strength. Then, just as suddenly, the noise subsided, only to repeat itself again and again.

"It's the siren," someone called out in the brief pause between blasts.

"Another air raid must be coming. We have to get to the shelter," said another voice.

Susan sat up in bed and groped around frantically for her tunic. Every bone in her body seemed to vibrate with the intensity of the siren. She could barely think. How will they ever find their way in this darkness? They had practiced several times that day, and while they were slow and rather noisy at first, by their last effort they were able to rise, dress, and silently make their way to the crypt within minutes. But all their practicing had been in daylight, when they were fully awake. Mother Gabriel had warned them that the raids might happen at night, when the Russians could use the cloak of darkness to protect their approach.

A dim ray of light split the darkness in half. Sister Agnes appeared with a flashlight. She hurried down the center aisle, swinging the light from side to side, momentarily illuminating each bed, allowing the girls a brief glimpse to orientate themselves. Susan spotted her tunic on the floor. She hoped that Vera, too, was getting ready.

Another volley of siren blasts sounded. Susan covered her ears against the piercing noise and hurried out into the hall where others were already making their way towards the kitchen. An icy wind blew through the open doorway. Susan felt her way around the edges of counters and tables, several times bumping into Anna in front of her.

"I'm sorry," she whispered each time, "I can't see where I'm going."

Susan shivered when she stepped outside the building. How could it be this cold? It had been such a beautiful fall day. They had completed all their practicing just wearing light sweaters. Now she wished for a regular winter coat. Susan counted the statues as they fled. It was when she reached the ninth one that the steady roar of a plane filled the silence of the night. A few seconds later, the first flare lit the sky with its eerie orange glow. She gasped in fright, feeling vulnerable and exposed in her tunic and sweater. Anyone peeking through the gates or looking down from the planes would surely see them.

"Get closer to the bushes and statues and keep moving," Sister Agnes whispered loudly from behind. They broke into a run. Susan's untied shoe flopped on her feet. At last she reached the church wall and disappeared behind the bush. With Anna, she squeezed through the narrow door and down a worn set of wooden stairs. A nun greeted them at the bottom and wrapped a wool blanket around them. She shooed them away from the doorway toward the opposite wall. Relieved that they had arrived safely and grateful for the unexpected blanket, Susan and Anna huddled together. Sister Magda appeared beside them with a thermos and a stack of cups.

"It's only water," she said cheerfully, "but it's hot." Susan wrapped her icy fingers appreciatively around the steaming cup. With her eyes, she searched the other blanketed bodies and quickly picked out Vera's golden curls. She, too, was cradling a mug of hot water.

Though she had seen the room earlier in the day while practicing, it had a different feel to it at night, and in the middle of an air raid. It was dimly lit by four large candles held in brackets along one of the stone walls. Three of the walls were made of large stones cemented together, but the wall adjacent to the door, on which the back of the church rested, was solid rock with large diagonal cracks through which water trickled and dripped to the dirt floor. The ceiling was low. Mother Gabriel, one of the tallest women there, had to walk with her head slightly bent. Narrow planks had been placed on crates around the room for seating.

As Mother Gabriel had promised, sheets fastened to supporting wooden pillars sectioned off the far end of the room. *That's where the caskets must be.* Susan shuddered at the thought, secretly thankful that Anna's question had prompted Mother Gabriel to have the barrier erected.

The weathered wooden door swung shut after the last person. A tense silence descended on the group as the thick stone walls blocked out all sound from the outside world.

"Let's begin by saying a little prayer," Mother Gabriel suggested. There was a low rumble from above. The nuns increased the volume of their prayer. It was only when they finished, and silence once again enveloped them, that Susan realized how comforting the steady rhythm of their prayer had been.

Another rumble, louder this time and followed by an enormous bang, caused the stone walls to tremble around them. Several muffled explosions followed. The younger girls began to cry in fear, and Susan hurried to Vera's side.

"Why don't we sing?" Sister Ibi called out with forced cheerfulness. Without waiting for approval, she started into a simple folk song. It had the desired effect. Immediately, several of the nuns and girls joined in. Soon, Vera's tears had dried and a weak smile flickered on her face as they sang the familiar tune. The only one who remained silent, Susan noticed, was Julia, who still stuck to her resolve not to sing again.

They sang until most of the nuns' repertoire was exhausted. But the fighting above ground continued. As they paused, trying to think of one more song, Susan had an idea.

"Why don't we sing a Jewish song?" she asked, looking from Mother Gabriel to Sister Agnes.

"Why of course," Mother Gabriel responded without hesitation. "But you girls will have to teach us the words." Susan, Ester, and several of the older girls led the nuns in a couple of Hebrew melodies. Again there was a pause.

"We haven't sung 'Hava Nagila' yet," Vera cried out. "We can even dance to that! We danced to this song at weddings and other celebrations Susan and I went to with Mama and Papa. And I even remember the easy steps." She jumped up and held out her arms expectantly. Anna, Ester, Susan, and Irene, exchanging glances, joined her. Sister Agnes, Sister Teresa, and Sister Ibi came over.

"Come on, we need more people," Vera jumped up and down excitedly. Slowly, others rose to join them.

"You all have to put your arms across each other's shoulders," Vera instructed, proudly in control, "and form a circle like this."

Vera led them around, side stepping, one foot gracefully crossing over the other, her body twisting and turning, setting the beat with her voice. Susan watched her little sister with admiration. She was born to dance. The song and steps were simple, and soon all the feet and voices followed along. At one point the dancers paused, drew into the center with arms raised, hands brushing the low ceiling, only to expand back out and then in again. The flickering candlelight cast a fairy glow on their movements. They repeated the pattern over and over again, each time moving faster and singing louder until they collapsed in a laughing, exhausted heap. They barely heard the single siren blast signaling the end of the raid.

One by one, first the nuns, then the girls, left the shelter and in a silent procession returned to the dormitory and the warmth of their beds.

It was only the next morning, on their way back from Mass, as the sun shed its first rays over the garden, that they noticed the destruction caused by the previous night's raid. Three large craters blemished the surface of the sloping garden. A bed of rose bushes had disappeared. The small turret in the middle of the roof had a gaping hole. The large cross, which had adorned it, was gone.

Yet, as Susan surveyed the damage and recalled the singing and dancing of the previous night, she was hopeful. They were still alive.

The bombings overhead broke convent windows and tore a hole in the roof.

Chapter 24

An Unwelcome Surprise

The following day, on November 4, Margit Bridge was accidentally blown up in the middle of the day killing hundreds of pedestrians. Tears welled in Susan's eyes as she remembered the good times her family had had there. *How will we get to the island now for our picnics?* she wondered.

After a few days, it seemed like the shelter beneath the church was becoming their second home. Susan was sure that they spent at least as much time there as they did in the convent. The air raids happened as frequently during the day as at night. The wailing sirens screamed at them, insisting that they drop everything and run.

Like some of its walls, the rigid routine of the convent crumbled. When sleep at night was impossible, they slept during the day. When

Father Markus failed to show up for the early morning service because it was too dangerous, they held it in the afternoon or evening and on some days not at all. Instead of arithmetic or grammar and poetry, the girls, even the youngest, learned to mend, cook, clean, and even, when it was safe, care for the sick. Nothing was predictable anymore except for the sporadic gunfire, the shouted commands and the sounds of alarm that rose up the hillside to the convent.

Throughout the month, the fighting within and around the city intensified as the Russians tried to gain a foothold in Budapest. Arrow Cross and Nazi soldiers constantly patrolled the streets, with their guns ready to shoot at any suspicious movement or sound.

Several new craters pockmarked the grounds, and much of the front left corner of the building lay in ruins. Boarded up windows that had been shattered by the force of bomb blasts dotted the convent walls. The nuns, with the help of the girls, did whatever temporary repairs they could in order to keep out the cold. Susan was surprised to see the deftness with which Sister Magda stirred a bucket of cement or sawed through a jagged piece of lumber.

"Just like mixing dough or slicing bread," Sister Magda winked at her.

But what impressed Susan the most was the nuns' courage.

They were nearing the end of Mass on a crisp, cold morning in late November when, once again, the dreaded sirens drowned out the priest's words. The nuns struggled to remain composed and attentive during the final minutes of the service before hurrying the girls to the safety of the shelter. Thankfully, the air raid, though very close, judging by the intensity of the blasts, was relatively brief this time.

They returned eagerly to the dining room where Sister Magda and her assistants greeted them with bowls of hot porridge. With their hunger appeased, Susan and Julia led a troop of girls toward their dormitory to start on their morning chores. They found Sister Agnes standing beside the door as though transfixed.

"Don't come any closer," she yelled, flinging her arms out to the side to guard against their advance. "Someone run and get Mother Gabriel." Julia ran down the hall. Another nun pushed her way through the throng of girls. She gasped as she came up beside Sister Agnes.

"How could this be?" she whispered when she saw what lay there. "What are we going to do?"

Despite Sister Agnes's warning, several of the girls drew closer. Susan peered around Anna's shoulder. A large green cylinder lay on the ground at the nun's feet. It was pointed at one end. Small metallic wings protruded from the other. It was almost as long as Vera.

"What is that?" Susan asked simultaneously with several others.

"I – I think it's a bomb – a bomb that hasn't exploded yet," Sister Agnes whispered back, as if she feared her voice might set the bomb off. "I can't imagine how it got here without exploding."

Mother Gabriel arrived and the girls parted to let her pass. She pressed her thin lips together and the lines in her forehead deepened as she considered the situation.

"Agnes," she said at length, "you must go out into the street and ask the soldiers on patrol if they would be kind enough to come in and remove a bomb for us."

"But the girls," Sister Agnes objected, still whispering. "What about our girls? They can't be seen."

"The girls," Mother Gabriel replied, encompassing them all with a commanding look, "will all return to the dining room where they will remain very quiet. This must be taken care of at once." As Sister Agnes hurried off, the rest of them turned to comply with Mother Gabriel's request. Susan felt a tug on her sleeve.

"Let's hide here and watch from behind this door," Julia whispered in her ear. She pulled Susan toward the older girls' dormitory across the hall. Anna pushed in beside them. Julia laid a slender finger against her lips.

"What if it explodes?" Susan whispered after several tense moments.

"We'll be blown into a million pieces," Julia said matter-of-factly. "No one will even know what became of us."

"Hush," whispered Anna, "look!" They crowded around the narrow opening. Sister Agnes was coming down the hall followed by Sister Teresa and three heavily armed soldiers. Two wore the Hungarian Arrow Cross uniforms, the third was clearly a German Nazi.

"What if they search the rooms?" Anna gasped, the color draining from her face. "What if they find us?"

"Quiet!" Julia hissed.

The soldiers arrived at the bomb. They looked at it in silence.

"*Nicht gut!*" the Nazi finally said. "It is not good. But there is nothing we can do. This requires an expert."

"It cannot be moved," one of the Arrow Cross soldiers explained to the nuns. "It is too dangerous. We are not experts. We might get blown up." He and the other two soldiers turned on their heels and marched back down the hall. Mother Gabriel hurried after them.

"Please," she begged. "You cannot leave it. What are we going to do?"

The Nazi soldier paused, frowning. "We can do nothing," he said in broken Hungarian. "If you are worried, *you* move it." He paused and for the first time looked around the hall, at Mother Gabriel and the other two nuns. "Who lives here? How many?" He barked the questions at them.

"Nuns live here." Mother Gabriel replied with a firm voice. "Not too many."

The German shrugged. "You should leave the mountain. It is too dangerous here for nuns." He turned to leave. This time, Mother Gabriel escorted them to the front door. When she returned, she was carrying a folded white sheet. She faced the two nuns.

"We'll have to remove the bomb ourselves," she said. "It cannot remain here. Once it is safely outside, a safe distance from the building, I will find a qualified person to deactivate it. We will not be inviting anymore Nazi soldiers to come inside the convent. Now, let's get to work." Sister Teresa and Sister Agnes exchanged frightened looks, but obediently followed Mother Gabriel back to the bomb where they all paused for a moment in silence.

"I bet they're praying," Anna whispered in Susan's ear.

The three nuns spread the sheet on the floor next to the bomb. Slowly, with great care, they lifted it and laid it gently on the sheet.

Judging by their strained expression, Susan figured that the bomb must be heavy. Probably thinking the same thing, Julia boldly stepped out from behind the door and hurried over to help. Sister Agnes gasped and Mother Gabriel opened her mouth as if to speak, but no sound came out. Instead, changing her mind, she nodded at Julia and pointed at one corner of the sheet. Julia grabbed hold, as did each of the nuns with their own corners. They wound the fabric securely around their wrists and lifted it off the ground. They worked in silence, communicating only through their eyes. They slowly turned and, with measured steps, moved down the hall. As they neared the doorway, Mother Gabriel called over her shoulders. "Susan, please run and open the doors for us."

Mother Gabriel must have guessed that she would be with Julia. There was no time to deliberate. Susan rushed to help.

The nuns and Julia descended the five steps leading from the front doors and then carefully made their way over to a large crater, the remnant of a previous attack. Susan and Anna, who had come up behind her, held their breaths as the nuns slowly let out some of the cloth, eased their way around the edge and gently positioned the loaded sheet over the crater. Bit by bit, they lowered the bomb into the crater until it came to rest on the bottom. At a nod from Mother Gabriel, they let the sheet fall in on top. Then, bending down, they sprinkled soft loose soil in the area immediately surrounding it. When at last they straightened up, Susan and Anna, heedless of the consequences, jumped up and down and cheered. Mother Gabriel smiled up at them and waved.

Chapter 25

Lena

Returning from the church on a bitterly cold, early December morning, the girls were once again talking about the bomb when Susan suddenly stopped. "Did you hear that?" she asked Anna.

"Hear what? I can't hear or see anything," said Anna, glancing around.

"It was coming from over there," said Susan, pointing, "from behind those bushes. Listen!" Both girls stood still, straining their ears.

Now they heard it clearly – a faint whimper from the bushes just uphill from where they stood.

"What is it?" asked Sister Agnes who had come up behind them. "Why aren't you girls going inside? It's freezing out here!"

Then she heard it, too. "Who is over there?" she asked, hurrying off the path as she spoke. "It sounds like someone is crying." She parted the dense branches, revealing the curled up form of a girl lying on the frozen ground. "Come here and help me," Sister Agnes called to Susan and Anna.

The girls rushed forward and reached down to help Sister Agnes draw out the shivering body of the young girl.

"It's a stranger," Susan cried out. "How did she get here?"

"We can ask questions later," said Sister Agnes, her voice heavy with concern. "Right now she obviously needs our help."

The girl stood up on shaky legs and leaned against Sister Agnes. She looked about Susan and Anna's age. Her long, black hair was matted together in clumps. Mud streaked over her dark-complexioned face. She wore an ill-fitting summer dress, torn and patched in several spots. The ragged blanket she clutched around her narrow shoulders as a shawl clearly gave her little warmth. Now that she was standing up, they saw that she was as tall as Sister Agnes, but very, very thin. On her stockingless feet, she wore an old pair of army boots, one with a gaping hole at the toe.

"Girls, I need your help," Sister Agnes said. "I don't think she can walk as far as the building. Anna, you run ahead and tell Sister Klara in the infirmary that we need her immediately. And have her prepare some warm blankets and hot water. Susan, help me lead this girl inside."

Not knowing whether she could trust the strange girl, Susan

hesitated for an instant. But Sister Agnes seemed not to care that the girl was a stranger. Julia's words flashed in her mind. *There is no time to be frightened when you focus on helping someone.* She reached out and put an arm around the girl's back, clasped hands with Sister Agnes beneath the girl's thighs, and they lifted her together. Susan was surprised at how light she was. After a few steps, the girl's head drooped onto Susan's shoulder. She cast a weak but grateful smile at Susan.

"What is your name, dear?" Sister Agnes asked gently.

There was a long pause before they heard a faintly whispered reply. "Lena."

"How did you get here?" asked Susan. "How long have you been out here? Where is your family?" Overwhelmed by her own curiosity, Susan's questions tumbled out, one after another. Lena opened her mouth to answer, but no sound came out. Her head rested heavier on Susan's shoulder, her eyes closed. Glancing at one another over her head, Susan and Sister Agnes increased their pace.

When they got inside, Sister Klara's stocky form bustled down the hall toward them. Her arms were laden with a blanket, a hot water bottle, and some clean clothes.

"Oh my, you poor dear," Sister Klara clucked, shaking her head when she saw Lena. She wrapped the blanket with the hot water bottle tucked inside around the trembling girl.

Lena's eyes opened wide as if surprised at this sudden kindness. She cast another grateful glance toward Susan before the nuns carried her off toward the infirmary.

During breakfast, there was much curious whispering among the girls about the young girl who was sleeping in the infirmary.

"She was just cold and hungry," explained Susan. "Probably like we would be if we weren't here."

"I wonder what happened to her," said Anna. "Perhaps she escaped from the ghetto that Julia told us about."

Julia, who had become one of Sister Klara's helpers in the infirmary, joined them at the table as they were finishing their breakfast. The girls turned to her expectantly.

"The new girl, Lena, is bathed and resting comfortably," she announced. "I helped Sister Klara cut her hair. There was no way we could brush out those tangles. I don't think Lena was very happy with that. But she doesn't look too bad now, except for her feet. Sister Klara said she has frostbite in two of her toes. And she's so thin!"

"Well, she's not going to get fat here," grumbled another girl scooping up a spoonful of watery gruel and letting it slop back into the bowl to illustrate her point.

"At least she'll get something to eat," replied Julia. "We aren't starving yet! Besides, I think Sister Magda has some kind of a surprise. She wouldn't allow me into the kitchen when I came to get some tea and cereal for Lena. She's only letting the nuns in there this morning."

"Perhaps I could go up and visit her," Susan suggested, but Julia told her that Lena was sleeping. She would have to wait.

When the girls returned to the dining room for their noontime meal, a strange aroma filled their nostrils. Anna took a deep breath.

"Smells like meat," she announced. "I can't remember the last time we had meat."

Sure enough, as soon as they had said grace, Sister Magda and her assistant nuns brought out steaming bowls of thick, aromatic stew, made mostly of meat with a few chunks of potatoes and onions.

Susan sniffed at her bowl suspiciously.

"It's horse meat stew," said Sister Magda proudly. "The Sisters told me the other day that it's what everybody in the city is eating these days. It's about the only way we can get fresh meat now. So yesterday when I heard that a couple of horses had been killed in the skirmish just down the street, I sent some of the Sisters out to carve a few big slabs for me."

It didn't take long for Susan and the others to overcome their initial revulsion at eating horse meat. It felt good to have a full stomach for a change.

"Susan," Julia stood, her empty bowl in her hand, "Do you want to help me take some of the stew up to Lena? She might be awake by now, and Sister Klara thought she should eat something nourishing."

"I'm coming too," announced Anna.

They went eagerly with Julia into the kitchen, helped assemble a tray of food, and followed Julia up the stairs to the infirmary.

Lena was sitting up in bed when they walked through the door. They could hear Sister Klara rummaging about in the storage room next door.

"Hi, Julia," Lena said when she saw them. She looked inquisitively at Susan and Anna. "I don't know your names." She had a lilting sing-song voice, and although she spoke in an unfamiliar Hungarian dialect, the girls could still understand. Susan had to pay close attention in order to catch everything she said.

"I'm Susan and this is Anna. How are you feeling?"

Lena gave them a tentative smile.

"So much better," she said, "and ever so warm." She wiggled her shoulders deeper into the extra wool blanket wrapped around her.

She did look a lot better, Susan thought. Her newly shortened, dark hair fell in soft wisps around her narrow face, accenting her large brown eyes. The white gown she wore contrasted strongly with her olive brown skin giving her a rather exotic appearance.

"Here, we brought you some food from the kitchen." Julia laid the tray on the small table beside the bed. "Sister Klara said the meat will help you get your strength back."

Lena swung her legs around the side of the bed, and Susan noticed her feet were swollen and a couple of her toes still had a purple hue.

"Are they sore?" Susan asked.

"Not really. They were at first, as they were warming up. But they're better now. Those toes," she said pointing to the purple ones, "I can hardly feel them at all. Sister Klara says I can try getting up after I've eaten some more. She's looking for some extra-large slippers. I hope she's right and that I couldn't walk before because I was so weak from hunger and cold – and not because of my feet. I can't stand the thought of not being able to move around."

"What were you doing in the garden?" Susan asked. She liked Lena's lively straight-forwardness and was eager to know more about her. "Where is your family? Where did you come from?"

Lena's animated face suddenly became solemn. "I don't know where my family is," she said softly. "It was the soldiers who took them away. They came to our camp at night and woke us up. No one had a chance to get away. Except for me."

"Your camp?" Susan, Anna, and Julia asked in unison. They looked at one another, confused.

"Do you mean the ghetto in the city where all the Jewish people are forced to live?" asked Anna. Lena shook her head.

"I don't know about any ghetto," she said. "I mean the camp – the Gypsy camp near the railroad yard just outside the city." Again the girls exchanged glances, but this time of understanding. Lena was a Gypsy.

"But why would the soldiers raid your camp?" asked Susan. "It's the Jewish people that they are rounding up."

"Everybody knows about the Jews and what is happening to them," said Lena, her voice quivering. "But the Nazis and those Arrow Cross soldiers are also after us Gypsies. They don't like anyone who is different from them. They took everyone from the camp, even old Gramps and Miz Jutka, who was going to have her baby any day." Lena's eyes filled with tears. "I have no idea where they are."

Susan regarded Lena thoughtfully. She had no idea that the Gypsies were being persecuted by the Nazis. *How many other groups of people were their victims?* she wondered.

Julia went to sit on the bed next to Lena and put her arms around the girl. "You will be safe here," she said. "These nuns take care of anyone who needs help. They don't care who you are." She reached for the bowl of stew they had brought for Lena. "Here, you had better start eating this before it gets cold." Lena wiped her eyes and eagerly took a mouthful of meat.

"This is an unusual place, isn't it?" Lena asked between slurping mouthfuls of the stew. "Those women look strange with those headdresses. And why are *you* here?" Again the girls looked at each other. How much of the truth could they trust to this Gypsy girl? But they didn't need to worry, for Lena went on without waiting for an answer.

"I've been running and hiding for days. While the Nazis were busy rounding up the others, I slipped out in the dark under the back flap of our shack." She shook her head at the memory. "I hoped that somehow I could help my people escape. But the Arrow Cross men were always around with their guns. I gave up when they put everyone on a train. I don't know where they took them."

There was an awkward moment of silence. Lena's story sounded so familiar. Her family had faced the same persecution that the Jewish families had. Perhaps it was safe to reveal to her who they were.

"The Nazis would like to get us, too," said Susan. "All of us girls here are Jewish. The nuns are hiding us."

"Do you think they will let me stay here, too?" Lena asked. "I've hidden in alleys and in barns and have had to steal my food whenever

I can. The trouble is nobody has much these days. But it was the cold that really got to me last night. I haven't been able to get any warmer clothes. When I saw those women bringing in the buckets of horsemeat and the gate wide open, I snuck in. It was a good thing I did, wasn't it? I'd like to stay here for a while. Do you think they'll let me?"

"Of course they'll let you stay," Susan reassured her. It made sense for Lena to stay. She needed to be hidden as much as they did. "The nuns like to help people. We all do," Susan added with a smile. "When your feet are better, we'll show you around and get you to meet every-one. You'll like it here."

Chapter 26

Christmas 1944

"We might not have enough food, but we sure have plenty of candles to light both a Chanukah menorah and a Christmas tree," Julia said to Susan and Lena as they were cleaning the sacristy of the church. A bomb had grazed the edge of the roof during a recent raid, and a few of the ancient bricks had fallen from beneath the ceiling, scattering dust and rubble over the small room. Once Mother Gabriel had decided that there was no more danger of falling bricks, she asked the girls to clean up the mess.

"Chanukah?" asked Lena, "What is that?" She had been at the convent for almost a week now and, though she still limped on her sore feet, she insisted on participating with the girls in all their various duties.

"It's a Jewish celebration, also called the Festival of Lights," Susan explained, pausing in the midst of lifting a freshly polished silver chalice back to its shelf. For the first time in her life, she had forgotten all about the holiday. "We light a candle every night for eight days, and sometimes we receive coins or a small gift on each day. It occasionally happens at the same time as Christmas, depending on the Jewish calendar." She adjusted the chalice on the shelf, squinting in order to catch the glint of its shiny surface. "But I guess we won't be celebrating anything this year," she added mournfully.

"Why not?" asked Lena. "Wouldn't the nuns want to celebrate Christmas no matter what? There are lots of pine trees in the garden. We could certainly have a Christmas tree. And," she paused for a moment, thinking, "we could make presents for all the younger children."

"Make presents?" both Julia and Susan said at once with raised eyebrows.

"How could we make presents here?" Susan continued. "What would we make them out of? We have nothing here." She recalled the carefully planned crafts she used to make with Mama at home. Now, she barely had paper for drawing. Dismissing Lena's suggestion, she reached for a candlestick and put a drop of silver polish on it. Methodically, she began smearing it with her cloth in ever larger circles on the smooth surface.

"You're wrong," insisted Lena. "There is so much here that we could use to make presents." She spread her arms wide. "We could make gifts for everyone. Anna could help too."

Susan's heart beat faster. Perhaps Lena was right. In the few days that Lena had spent among them, they had already learned that she was full of ideas and very skilled with her hands. Right now, she was carefully gluing back together a small statue that had been shattered by one of the falling bricks.

"So, what can we make?" asked Susan. "And do you think we could make something for the nuns as well? They have done so much for us."

For the next couple of weeks, Susan, Anna, Lena, and Julia occupied themselves with their special project during every spare minute. From Mother Gabriel, they got permission to establish their workshop in one of the small storage rooms in the basement. Under Lena's guidance, they collected dried chestnuts, acorns, and sticks from the grounds. They hunted through the nuns' scrap bins for fabric, ribbon, thread, yarn, and they found other decorative baubles lying around. Then, with great patience, Lena showed Susan, Julia, and Anna how to make little stick dolls with acorns for heads and wrinkled horse chestnuts for bodies. She taught them to stitch tiny outfits and braid strands of yarn for hair. For the older girls, they embroidered longer bits of cloth to serve as hair ribbons. For the nuns, they made bookmarks. Susan drew patterns or pictures of flowers on strips of paper, which Lena then filled in with colorful pieces of fabric. They framed some of Susan's drawings of the garden with straight strips of bark to give to Mother Gabriel.

"Don't these look better than anything we could have bought in a store?" Susan asked, proudly examining their creations.

To everyone's delight, Christmas Eve was ushered in by the first real snowfall of the winter. The garden was blanketed in white, sparkling snow when they stepped out of the church after the special Christmas Mass that evening. The clear, fresh air in her lungs, the twinkling stars overhead, and the faint clanging of distant church bells almost made Susan feel that the world was at peace.

The living-room doors were shut, with Mother Gabriel standing guard, when the girls arrived back inside the convent. She waited until everyone had crowded into the hallway before she spread the doors wide open. There was a brief moment of stunned silence before the "oohs" and "ahhs" of the girls as they poured into the candlelit room and spread out around the majestic Christmas tree that stood in front of the windows. It was adorned with a shining star on top. The fresh smell of pine permeated the room. The tree was decorated with candles and colorful glass balls, garlands of silver, and angel's hair that the nuns kept from year to year.

"Merry Christmas, Merry Christmas," the nuns called repeatedly as they went around hugging all the girls.

Later, as the girls and nuns sat cradling steaming cups of hot cocoa and freshly baked buns, which Sister Magda had conjured up from somewhere, Susan, Lena, Julia, and Anna walked in with several large baskets, brimming with gifts. Proudly, they distributed their treasures among the gaping girls and nuns.

"Look at my doll! Look at my doll!" Vera ran over to Susan. "Don't you think Mama would like it?"

"Let me see." Susan reached for Vera's doll, not wanting her little sister to know that she was the one who had made it, taking special care over every detail.

"I know you made my book mark," Sister Agnes said to Susan. "It's the only one decorated with carrots and onions and potatoes instead of flowers. Who else would have thought of doing that? It is very special to me. Thank you."

"Thank you, too," Susan said awkwardly, twisting her new hair ribbon around her fingers. "Thank you for letting me work in the garden with you."

Watching the nuns and the girls open their presents, Susan's heart was filled with joy. To think that she had helped make this happen! She searched for Lena's smiling face. And if she hadn't met Lena, none of this would have happened. Somehow – in the midst of the terrible war and all their worries – they were able to bring laughter and happiness into this day.

"You girls have managed to give us something very valuable," Sister Agnes embraced Susan, "when even we thought there was nothing left to give."

Christmas Eve turned out to be a short-lived oasis of peace. The very next day the Russians succeeded in surrounding the city of Budapest, cutting it off from the rest of the world. The situation for the Nazis became desperate and they quickly intensified their efforts to find and eliminate the Jews in the city. The convent, with Nazis positioned above and beside them, suffered the consequences.

Chapter 27

The Raid

December 27, 1944

"Hurry girls, hurry!" Sister Agnes's voice was as loud as a whisper would permit without trespassing the borderline of silence. She stood with her back to the dormitory door, holding it open with the full force of her slight body. With one arm, she beckoned. With the other, she gently guided the sleepy bodies from the room into the dimly lit hallway.

Obediently, Susan shuffled behind the white-clad bodies in front of her. She was confused. There had been no shrill blast of the siren this time, alerting them to danger. There was no hum of approaching planes threatening to drop their bombs over the sleeping city. The distant cannons above them on the mountain top were silent. Instead, each of them had awakened to the hushed voice of Sister Agnes urging them to get out of bed. With a slight gesture of her hand, she had signaled to the girls to leave their neat piles of clothes untouched at the foot of their beds. No time for getting dressed this time.

They had made this nighttime journey dozens of times in response to the sirens. But now, instead of the siren's wail, Susan heard banging and shouting coming from the direction of the front doors. She passed Vera's room and glanced in through the open door. The pale light from the partly obscured moon outside the window cast a dim glow. The covers on all thirty beds had been thrown back haphazardly. As far as Susan could see, every one of them was empty. Relieved, Susan followed the stream of girls.

She was halfway down the hall when suddenly she picked up her pace and forced her way to the front of the line. There she stopped and carefully scrutinized each form as it passed her. It was very hard to see in the dark hallway, to make out who was who. Still, by the time Sister Agnes appeared behind the last of the girls, Susan was sure.

"Vera is not here," she told the nun.

The banging and the chorus of incomprehensible shouting from below intensified.

"What's happening?" asked Susan.

"It's the Nazis. They want to search the convent. We must hurry to the shelter. They will break through those doors any time now."

"But Vera, she's not here," repeated Susan.

"Nonsense," said Sister Agnes and she tugged at Susan's sleeve to pull her along. "I looked in all the rooms. Every bed was empty. I checked. You probably just missed seeing her. It's so dark in here."

"No. I was watching. She wasn't with them. I'm going back. I have to get Vera!"

"I'm sure there was no one left behind. I locked all the doors." Sister Agnes lightly rattled the keys dangling from her waist to prove her point. "Vera is so tiny. You could easily have missed her behind one of the taller girls. Come!" Susan heard the desperation in Sister Agnes's voice.

"No!" Susan yanked her arm free of Sister Agnes's grasp. "I didn't miss her." The two stared at each other. Susan, too, felt desperate. She was certain about Vera. Vera did not go down that hall!

Susan turned on her heels and ran back down the corridor.

"Susan! The doors, I – " Sister Agnes's voice was drowned out by the cracking of splintering wood and the yelling and pounding from outside.

Susan covered the distance down the gloomy hallway in no time, focusing her eyes on the small rectangle of dim light shining through the window in the dormitory's door.

When she reached the door and pushed down on the ancient handle, it held fast against her.

She rattled the door, desperately trying to see beyond the pane of frosted glass. "Vera, are you in there?" she banged on the door with her fist. "Vera!" She dared not raise her voice any louder.

"Vera!" Susan kicked at the door.

In the distance, she heard the splintering of wood. The main doors were breaking!

In a burst of panic, her fist flew through the thin window pane.

Shards of glass dug into the tender flesh of her wrist as she pulled it back. She bit her lips together, reached through the gaping hole to the lock on the other side and opened the door. Jagged points sliced her arm. The thin, white sleeve of her nightgown turned a deep red.

"Vera, are you there? Can you hear me?" Susan jumped lightly over the shattered pane and ran to Vera's bed, half way down the long room, thankful for the silvery beam of moonlight that lit her way. As Sister Agnes had said, Vera's bed was empty like all the others. But Susan knew her little sister well. She walked around to the far side of the bed, ducked down, and peered into the gloom beneath. Near the head of the bed, blocked from sight by one of the low wooden cabinets that separated the beds from one another, was a large bundle. With her unhurt left arm, Susan reached out and touched it. She recognized the texture of the rough woolen blanket that covered each bed. There was something firm and warm within the blanket. Susan shook the bundle. She pulled on the blanket and dragged it with its content from beneath the bed.

"Vera, wake up! We have to get out of here."

"Leave me alone. I'm not going anywhere. I want to sleep," her faint voice grumbled back. Susan tugged at the blanket.

"Get up, Vera. The Nazis are breaking in. We have to run to the shelter."

"There was no siren. It can't be a real raid. And it's cold."

"It's not an air raid this time. It's the Nazis. They're at the gates. That's why there was no siren. No warning. Now come on!" As if to prove Susan's point, there was another loud cracking sound of wood breaking apart. Vera popped up into a sitting position, her eyes wide with fright, her mouth hanging open, speechless.

"Let's go!" Susan grabbed hold of Vera's hand, pulling the younger girl up. But as she stood herself, her blood-soaked gown stuck against her body, Susan felt the room tilt around her. Her legs felt weak. She grasped the bed frame for support.

"What are those red blotches on your gown?" Vera asked, straining her eyes to see in the dim light.

"It's just a bit of blood. I cut myself on some glass. I'll be fine," she said, reassuring both herself and Vera. "Sister Agnes is waiting. She'll take care of us. Come on, please, let's go." Susan tugged on Vera's arm, hoping she sounded stronger than she felt. Holding on to each other, they hurried down the length of the room.

As they reached the doorway, they almost collided with Sister Agnes.

"Oh, Susan, I'm so sorry," she exclaimed, clasping her hand to her chest. "But look at you! What have you done?" With a swift motion she grabbed a towel and wrapped it around Susan's right shoulder and arm.

"This will do for now," she said. She hastily wiped the blood off the floor with a sheet and stuffed it under the mattress. She placed a firm arm around Susan's shoulder and pulled the two girls back down along the hall.

"You took so long," Sister Agnes explained as they retraced their steps, "that I came to look for you. I think they have broken in. We can't waste any time. We must get to the shelter." They slipped through the door to the stairwell.

At last, they reached the kitchen.

"I wish I had the key to lock this door behind us," said Sister Agnes. "But only Sister Magda has it." They groped their way around the eerie shadows of suspended pots, ladles, and other cooking utensils to the far door leading out into the garden. It had been left slightly ajar and the chill night air streamed in. The footsteps, banging, and yelling were getting closer.

"Quickly, girls," Sister Agnes whispered, giving them a gentle shove toward the door. "Get over to the shelter."

Susan whipped around.

"What about you? Aren't you coming with us?"

"Yes, yes. I'll be with you soon. I'm just going to slow them down a bit," Sister Agnes said, distracted by the mounting noise. "We can't have them coming through the door after us. Hurry up now! And keep going till you are in the shelter. Don't wait for me. I'll come as soon as I can." The boots and voices were coming down the stairs.

"But…" Susan began.

"Go! They mustn't see you!" Sister Agnes whispered desperately as she pushed the two girls through the door.

"But it's still dark. We have never gone across at night by ourselves before," Vera pleaded. The doorknob at the far end of the kitchen began to turn.

"You won't be by yourselves," Sister Agnes said, her voice getting more and more desperate. "Your guardian angels are always with you."

Sister Agnes gave them a final push outside and shut the door firmly behind them.

Chapter 28

Running

O utside, Susan and Vera stood mesmerized for a moment. The garden stretched silently before them. Yesterday, they had been disappointed that the snow was melting. Now, Susan was thankful that it didn't leave telltale footprints for the soldiers to detect. The white crushed stones of the path lay exposed in front of the two girls.

They had traversed the garden many times in the middle of the night. But, in all those previous escapes to the shelter, Vera and Susan had been shepherded by the nuns who made sure none of their charges strayed from the path. This time, they were alone. It was dark and cold. Susan would have welcomed even the eerie yellow glow cast by the flares.

From behind the door, they suddenly heard the muffled shout of one of the soldiers.

"The Jews! Where are the Jewish girls? We have been informed that there are Jewish girls here."

"There are no Jewish girls in here. You are mistaken." They heard Sister Agnes's firm response.

Who would have informed the soldiers? Would they believe Sister Agnes? Or would they see the door and come searching in the garden? They had to get away! Susan's mind was reeling.

"Come quickly, Vera!" Susan grabbed her sister's hand and sprang onto the path. The damp ground numbed their bare feet. In their hurry, they had forgotten their slippers. Inside the towel, her hand and arm throbbed where the blood still oozed from her cuts.

In less than a minute, their steps slowed. How different the place looked when they were on their own in the dark! Now each tree trunk appeared to be a soldier, each bush an evil beast ready to pounce. The occasional drift of snow off the branches overhead gave the illusion of people moving in the shadows.

"Look," Vera whispered, pulling on Susan's gown. She pointed to the first white statue. In the surrounding darkness, it was a clear, reassuring landmark.

"Let's go," Susan said with renewed courage. "We can see our way from one statue to the next." The girls hurried silently forward past the first two statues. At the third, they paused. A sharp bend in the path hid the next statue from view.

"I'm so cold," whimpered Vera. "And there's something stuck in my heel."

"Why isn't Sister Agnes coming?" Susan muttered. "We have to get to the shelter! Surely – "

The loud sound of a rifle silenced her. It echoed off the surrounding hills. There was another shot, and then another. Susan's eyes searched the night for any hint of movement. She strained her ears for the sound of approaching steps. But all was quiet.

The deserted, winding path no longer seemed threatening compared to the menace behind them. The dark clusters of trees and bushes now beckoned as a safe haven.

"We have to run now," Susan tugged at her sister's arm. "Go!"

In their panic, the girls forgot about the cold, about aching hands and feet. The path grew steeper and rockier as they mounted the hill toward the church. "Five, six, seven…" Susan counted as they passed each group of stone figures. The distance between the convent and the church, which before had always seemed so short, now appeared infinite. "Only three more statues," she reassured Vera as they paused for a moment to catch their breath.

"I can't go any further. I can't feel my feet anymore." Vera's words came in short gasps.

"We can't stop now!" Susan tugged at Vera's arm. "Once they realize there is no one left in the building, the Nazis will come outside to the church. We have to get to the crypt. Here, I'll give you a piggyback ride." Susan turned her back to Vera and bent down.

"Ow! Oh, be careful!" Susan involuntarily gasped in pain as Vera jumped up and pressed against her cut arm. She bit her lips together to keep from crying out again. They were so close! She had to make it.

In that instant, the slam of the kitchen door echoed through the silence.

"They're out!" Vera hissed into Susan's ear as heavy German voices surrounded them. In the stillness of the night, it was difficult to tell the distance of the sounds.

Susan shifted Vera's weight slightly on her back and plunged forward once again. She struggled up over the final steep ascent to the church. Despite the cold, beads of sweat formed on her forehead. The shadowy forms of trees and bushes swam in front of her eyes. Her right arm felt strangely numb, and by the coldness of the gown against her skin, she knew that her whole side must be damp with her blood. The shouts of the Nazis were definitely closer now. They came from all directions.

At last, the massive form of the church stood before them. Vera let go of Susan's shoulders and dropped to the ground running to the bushes that concealed the door to the shelter of the crypt. Susan stumbled after her.

The girls had barely reached the safety of the bushes when they heard the crunch of stiff leather boots. It was frightfully near. Instinctively, they pressed their bodies close to the church wall. The wooden door was only an arm's length away, but they dared not move. The boots came closer. If only their gowns weren't so white. And where was Sister Agnes?

The steps paused just on the other side of the bush. Boots scuffled in the dirt. The narrow beam of a flashlight searched the bushes, trees, and grounds around them. It passed over their feet and paused. For an instant, it returned, shone directly on their feet again, then quickly flickered away focusing on the path the girls had just left.

Other boots came up. Deep German voices engaged in a brief argument. All the boots turned and retreated toward the front entrance of the church.

Susan heard the creaking of the doors, and then the chanting of the nuns at prayer poured out into the night. She understood at once. Most of the nuns must have gone to the church instead of the shelter. That would explain the emptiness of the convent building. To the soldiers, this might appear as a routine midnight worship.

Behind the bush, Susan forced herself to wait for another eternal moment. She made sure that none of the soldiers had remained behind before she allowed Vera to lunge for the door.

Susan and Vera stumbled down the rough stone steps into the waiting arms of a nun.

"I don't know where Sister Agnes is. I don't think she came after us," Susan managed to whisper before she fainted.

Chapter 29

Remembering

Susan lay on her back, eyes closed. Her arms, legs, her entire body blended blissfully with the warmth and softness of the bed. Something was not quite as it should be, but she did not know what it was.

She remembered being in the shelter, in the middle of the night, surrounded by a crowd of whispering girls. It should be dark, damp, and cold. Instead, she felt the warmth of the sun's rays dancing on her eyelids. A deep, heavy silence enveloped her. The warmth, the sun, the silence – it was all wrong. She didn't want to open her eyes. The effort was too great. She would wait just a little bit longer. At least, they were safe. She had brought Vera to the shelter.

She remembered finding Vera under the bed, Sister Agnes pushing them out through the kitchen door, their desperate flight across the garden, the sound of the soldier's boots, the opening of the shelter door.

Suddenly, she felt the gentle touch of a soft warm hand on her forehead.

Her eyes opened and she looked up into the kindly, wrinkled face of Sister Klara.

"Is this the infirmary?" Susan asked in wonder. Since her arrival at the convent, though she had frequently helped out here, she had never been a patient herself. "Why am I here?" But, as she tried to raise herself on her arm, before the nun had a chance to answer, she felt the pain of her many cuts. Her head sank back onto her pillow.

"Yes," Sister Klara nodded at her with approval. "Why don't you rest a bit longer. You gave us quite a fright," Sister Klara shook her head, "fainting the minute you entered the shelter." Sister Klara placed a cool, damp cloth on Susan's forehead. "I would faint, too, if I had lost so much blood." Sister Klara clucked her tongue and shook her head at Susan. "Breaking that dormitory window with your bare hands! At least that's what we figured from what Vera told us and the glass splinters in your arm." Her face clouded over.

She shook her head again and sighed. "Soon you will have to sit up and stand on your own two feet. Of course, I'll be right here to help. I wouldn't ask this so soon, but it can't be helped. You'll have to try to get there on your own. It's only right that you should be there." Sister Klara pressed her lips together and shook her head again.

Sister Klara's words made no sense to Susan. *Where would she have to "get to"? Where did she have to be?* Usually Sister Klara insisted that her patients remain in bed no matter what the danger. Slowly she turned her head to look more directly at the nun.

"Where – where do I have to go?" She asked reluctantly, not sure if she was ready to listen to another of Sister Klara's long tirades. "And where is everybody? It is too quiet here. Vera, is Vera all right? Where is she?"

Susan stopped abruptly as she noticed the trembling of Sister Klara's chin. The nun's eyes filled with tears and she buried her head in her hands. Her shoulders shook, and from time to time a sob, almost a hiccup, escaped from her lips.

Sister Klara was completely overcome by sorrow. There was nothing Susan could do but watch.

"It's not Vera, is it?" She asked finally, in a small, frightened voice. "Vera is alright, isn't she?"

Sister Klara took a deep, shuddering breath, wiped her eyes, and looked at Susan.

"I'm sorry, dear. I shouldn't have cried like that," she said quietly. "Vera is fine. She is at breakfast with the other girls. It's Sister Agnes. She is no longer with us. They killed her, those wicked soldiers! They shot her right outside the dormitory door. Oh, it is so horrible!" Sister Klara shook her head again, as if to rid her mind of the dreadful image. She made a quick sign of the cross over her chest.

"But she said she would follow right behind us," Susan objected, not wanting to acknowledge the reality of Sister Klara's words. "She was right there at the kitchen door with us. She couldn't have been by the dormitory. It can't be true." But even as she spoke, she recalled again the frightening night, their anxious waiting for Sister Agnes, her confusion as to why the nun was not coming. Then, the sound of gunshots.

"I'm afraid she must have led the soldiers back to the dormitory. Probably to detain them, to keep them from following you. Perhaps they forced her to. We will never know."

"She told us to go ahead to the shelter. She said she would just slow the soldiers down a bit. She said she would follow us…." Susan couldn't continue as tears choked her voice. Sister Klara wrapped an arm around Susan and pulled her close.

"Well now," she said. "It is very hard to lose someone, hard to know that we will never see them again. But we must remember that Sister Agnes is in heaven now. Sister Agnes died protecting you, protecting all the girls. Think of how much she loved you."

Susan wept quietly as Sister Klara talked. She recalled that last time when she looked into Sister Agnes's eyes by the kitchen door. She remembered the nun's firm determination to send them on their way and to stay behind. She must have realized then what the outcome of her action might be. Yet she courageously chose to stay.

"There will be a small funeral for Sister Agnes today. Mother Gabriel saw a large group of soldiers leave the house next door this morning and descend into the city. She said we must take advantage of this time while we can all gather safely in the church." Sister Klara stood up abruptly, trying to regain her composure.

"It would be good if you had the strength to come. I know you and Sister Agnes had a special friendship. Here is some hot cocoa and bread that Sister Magda sent up for you. And here are your clothes," she said, placing a small tray of food on the end table beside Susan and laying her tunic on the bed.

"You lost a fair bit of blood from your cuts, but I believe I have bandaged you up well. Do you think you could try to eat a bit now and then dress yourself?"

Susan nodded and wiped her eyes. She swung her legs around the side of the bed.

Sister Agnes was dead! *You and Sister Agnes had a special friendship*, Sister Klara had just said. She was right. Susan considered Sister Agnes a friend, more than an adult who took care of her. Their difference in age and religion had made little difference to their friendship.

Susan sighed. For a while now, she had forgotten to think about religious differences – her being Jewish and the nuns being Catholic. Somehow it didn't seem to matter anymore. They were all too busy trying to survive.

The sweet, tantalizing aroma of the cocoa made her head spin. She hadn't realized how hungry she was. Sister Agnes was dead, and here she was so easily distracted by her hunger. How could she be so heartless? But she bit into the thick slice of bread that by some miracle Sister Magda had conjured up from their meager food supply. It was spread thinly with peach jam. The fresh smell and flavor of the jam vividly brought back those hot summer days when, weary from weeding, she and Sister Agnes sat in the shade of the fruit tree, each eagerly devouring a large juicy peach. This jam was probably made from their harvest of fruit and secretly hoarded by Sister Magda for an emergency such as this.

Who will take care of the garden now? Who will be in charge of the little girls? Susan sighed and her salty tears mingled with the sweetness of the jam in her mouth.

Chapter 30
Ave Maria

Accompanied by Sister Klara and holding Vera's hand, Susan entered the church for Sister Agnes's funeral service on unsteady feet. Everyone was already assembled, sitting silently as if waiting just for them. As they walked in, all heads turned. Susan wondered if they thought this was all her fault – that Sister Agnes had died because she had gone back for Vera. But what else could she have done? She needed to protect her sister as she had promised.

As she looked into each pair of eyes she passed, Susan was relieved to find that there was no blame in any of them. Both the nuns and the girls, though overcome by sorrow, gave her small encouraging smiles. Everyone knew how attached she had been to Sister Agnes.

At the head of the center aisle, at right angles to the altar, lay a simple closed wooden coffin. One red rose lay on top. Without taking her eyes off the coffin, Susan slid into a pew next to Anna. Vera let go of her hand and hurried two rows toward the front to sit with Irene and the other younger girls.

Anna squeezed Susan's hand in greeting. Sister Teresa, from the row behind, leaned forward and embraced her.

Father Markus entered the sanctuary, and they all rose as the funeral for Sister Agnes began.

The Mass progressed like all the others, and soon Susan's attention wandered as the now-familiar Latin prayers filled her ears.

When Father Markus finished his sermon, he invited Mother Gabriel to say a few words. The creases on the Mother Superior's face showed her overwhelming sorrow. With a tremor in her voice, she spoke of her first meeting with Sister Agnes, the young nun's arrival at the convent, the work she did with the young girls. She spoke about Sister Agnes's love for growing things, her dedication to her vocation, and the children in her care. Above all, the Mother Superior praised her ability to sacrifice herself for others.

Next, a man from the front pew went up and awkwardly introduced himself as Sister Agnes's brother. In broken sentences, choked by emotion, he recalled memories of their childhood, how different they were, how he had teased her relentlessly, and finally his love for his sister who had remained a mystery to him.

A long silence followed after he sat down. Only sniffles and the soft rustling of cloth as trembling hands rummaged for handkerchiefs could be heard. Finally, at Father Markus's prompting, they all stood up. The nuns recited a prayer. Then in strong unfaltering voices, they sang the hymn "Ave Maria" together. "*Ave Maria, gratia plena …*" the words rang out.

As Susan listened to the first notes of the hymn – whose words they all knew now through frequent repetition – she heard a distinctly beautiful voice transforming the hymn into a spiritual experience. It was clear and steady, quiet at first but gradually growing in depth. All heads turned to the source of the singing. The nuns fell silent in wonder.

Julia, her strong soprano voice growing more and more powerful with each note, resonating from the highest corners of the church, sang out her gift of thanksgiving to Sister Agnes.

Part Four
Waiting

Chapter 31

A New Year

January 1945

December 31, 1944, was the saddest New Year's Eve that Susan had ever experienced. They had all hurried to the shelter just an hour before midnight when the dreaded siren screamed. There, clustered around the feeble glow of a few candles, and to the background sounds of the battle raging above ground, the nuns led them in prayer for peace in their country and in the world, for the safety of their families, and for some relief from their more immediate lack of food and heat. No one suggested singing or dancing. The absence of Sister Agnes was keenly felt by all.

The last days of December had been bitterly cold. Fuel, as well as food, had become increasingly scarce. The man who once brought their weekly coal supply with his rickety horse and wagon stopped making the rounds. Though the nuns had been very frugal in their use of fuel, it was clear that their preciously hoarded coal would not last much longer. Instead, they burned wood whenever they could find it. They burned any pieces of lumber they could pry loose from the rubble of destroyed walls. Mother Gabriel instructed them to remove any unnecessary doors and burn them. She even began eyeing the convent's furniture, especially the old school desks that for the time being were sitting idle. The girls spent a great part of each day, whether in the convent or the shelter, huddled together in groups of two or three, reading quietly to each other or playing word games under blankets.

Susan spent much of their confined time sketching pictures that she had stored in her mind – especially memories of Sister Agnes. At first, Susan's arm was weak and sore from her accident, and she had to rest often. But with Sister Klara's constant fussing over her bandages, she healed quickly.

After Sister Agnes's funeral, Mother Gabriel had given Susan a "pad" of drawing paper. "Before she died, Sister Agnes requested more drawing paper for you," Mother Gabriel told Susan. "She felt it was important for you to describe everything through your pictures. Because paper is so scarce now, she removed sheets of blank paper from the front and end of many books."

Susan's "pad" was made of sheets of varying sizes and textures. But the important thing was that, thanks to Sister Agnes's thoughtfulness, Susan could draw again. She hadn't had the luxury of paper for a long time, and she wanted these new drawings on her special pad to be the best she ever did – in honor of Sister Agnes.

She pictured the nun in the library and drew her face framed by that funny headdress, peeking around the massive library door. She drew a picture of a tiny Sister Agnes kneeling on the ground with a circle of gun barrels aiming down at her. As she drew, Susan recalled the many details of their times together. Her sense of loss lifted bit by bit as she transposed each scene, from her memory to paper.

On the first day of the new year, the morning light revealed a new calamity. A bomb had created yet another crater in the front garden and had destroyed the underground pipes that brought water into the convent. Now there was no running water for washing, for making tea, coffee, or any other meager cooking that Sister Magda had planned for the day. But, thankfully, it was winter. It had snowed for the past few days and, after their breakfast of dry slices of bread in the cold dining room, they all went outside and filled buckets and pots with piles of clean white snow.

"I never thought I would be thankful for snow," said Sister Magda, winking at Susan as she brought in yet another two buckets full.

"It's going to take forever to melt enough snow for us," Susan complained. "A full bucket only ends up as a few centimeters of water. And this water is so dirty! Where did all the dirt come from?" she asked, as she peered into the large pot.

"The dirt is always there," sighed Sister Magda. "We just couldn't see it because there was so much more of the white. I will pour the water through a strainer and boil it. And you don't need to worry about how little water one pot of snow ends up making. Look outside the window, it's snowing again. We might not have enough water to keep our clothes clean, but we won't die of thirst."

Even with all their difficulties, the girls knew that they were fortunate to be here within the convent walls. One day, when Susan and Julia were tidying the infirmary's storage room for Sister Klara, Mother Gabriel brought to the infirmary one of the younger nuns who worked in the city. She was crying and gasping for air, trying to talk at the same time.

"I'm never going out there again," she wailed repeatedly as Mother Gabriel and Sister Klara tried to comfort her. "They're killing all the Jews," she blurted out between big heaving sobs. Julia and Susan stopped in the doorway of the storage room, horrified by the nun's words. The others were oblivious to their presence.

"Hush, my dear," Mother Gabriel said. "You can tell us later. Don't worry, we won't send you out again. I'm sorry, it was my mistake." The nun looked at Mother Gabriel with a blotched, tear-stained face.

"Can't we do something to stop them? They are killing Jewish people by the hundreds, lining them up along the Danube and shooting them in the back. The river is red with blood. They are murdering children as well as the adults. Is there nothing we can do?" she asked again.

Mother Gabriel wrapped her arms around the young woman and gently leaned her head against her breast.

"We are doing as much as we can with our girls here," she consoled her. "Our job is to protect them and not do anything that might endanger their lives. The Nazis are getting desperate. They know their days are numbered, and they will be retreating soon." The nun nodded her head in agreement.

It had been almost seven weeks since the Russian army surrounded the city of Budapest on Christmas day. The girls woke to an earth-shattering noise and trembling walls and floors. Again, there had been no warning siren.

"What is happening this time? Is it an earthquake?" someone yelled. Everyone leapt screaming from their beds. They ran down the dark hallway in all directions, bumping into each other.

The nuns who left the convent each day to help others had to face the reality of what was happening.

Elizabeth Bridge was bombed (top) and then rebuilt after the war (bottom).

"Girls, walk! Calm down!" Sister Teresa, who was now in charge, yelled over the heads of the panic-stricken girls. Her voice went unheeded when, after a few moments, there was another blast and then another. Mother Gabriel appeared by the stairs with two other nuns, each holding a candle in their hands. They waited silently for the commotion to die down, as all eyes turned toward the source of light.

"It's not a raid and we are not under attack," Mother Gabriel said shaking her head. Her face had a strange, unearthly look as it appeared to hover in mid air above the flickering flame. "There is no need to panic. I just heard the news on the radio." For the first time, her usually calm and commanding voice quivered with excitement. "The Nazis are retreating. They are blowing up the bridges that cross the Danube so that the Russians won't follow."

There was a moment of stunned silence as the true meaning of Mother Gabriel's words began to sink in. All at once the entire group of girls, from the oldest to the youngest, were cheering, crying, laughing, jumping up and down, and hugging each other, all at the same time. Other nuns entered the already crowded hallway, smiling at the pandemonium.

Susan's heart beat rapidly. She grasped Anna's hand. They looked with a mingling of disbelief and eager anticipation into each other eyes.

"We'll be going home soon!" they shouted in unison.

Chapter 32

Good-byes

"How come no one is coming for us? When are *we* going home?" Vera's whining was becoming annoying as the days and then weeks went by.

"I thought you were happy here," Susan tried to avoid answering Vera's questions directly. "Aren't you helping Sister Teresa clean the rubble out of the old classroom and making it usable again? You wouldn't want to leave before that's all finished, would you?"

"But we don't belong here anymore," Vera pouted, giving a shake to her long golden curls. "Mostly everyone else is gone, even Irene. There's no one my age left to play with."

Susan sighed. Vera was right. Most parents, close relatives, or friends of the family had already come – some within days of the Nazi departure – to collect their girls and take them back home. Julia, Susan, and Vera where among the few remaining.

Anna and her sister Panni had been among the first to leave. Their mother came for them just days after the Nazi retreat. She told them her building had been marked by a yellow star and designated as a Jewish building. Several families were forced to move in with her, crowding her small apartment. But those families had moved out now, and she wanted her girls back home.

She told them tearfully that their father had been sent to a labor camp and she had not heard from him at all. When she asked to see Sister Agnes, there was an uncomfortable silence.

"You, you can't," Anna stammered. "She's gone."

"Gone? What do you mean gone?" Mrs. Dobos exclaimed. "I must see her. I have a message for her from the wife of that kind man, Viktor Majori, who helped you get in here. She wanted to let Sister Agnes know that he was taken to a labor camp when the Arrow Cross discovered that he was helping the Jews." Mrs. Dobos dabbed her eyes with one hand. "Mrs. Majori hasn't heard from him since. She is so distraught, poor woman! And she has all those children to look after. Now it's our turn to help her out."

"Well, we can certainly help her with her children," said Anna, hugging her mother. "We learned a lot about looking after small children and cooking and – "

"But I must speak with Sister Agnes," Mrs. Dobos interrupted. "Mrs. Majori wanted her to say prayers for her husband. Where has she gone?" She looked questioningly at the girls standing around her.

Before they could answer, Sister Teresa came to their rescue. She stepped forward and took both of Mrs. Dobos' hands in her own. "I'm sorry to have to tell you this, but Sister Agnes is dead. There was a raid..."

Susan, who had been watching the whole exchange between Anna, Panni, and their mother, turned away. The news that Mrs. Dobos brought about Viktor made her head throb. Viktor Majori was punished for helping Jews. What about Aunt Isi? They hadn't heard from her once since they arrived here. Julia said Aunt Isi had suddenly stopped bringing food to the ghetto. Perhaps she was also discovered helping Jews and had been taken to a camp.

Susan and Anna bid each other a hasty goodbye. Anna tried to reassure Susan that her turn to leave would come soon. After a promise to meet again, Anna was gone.

Every day after that, Susan watched anxiously through the dormitory windows trying to catch a glimpse of the street. She found herself walking more and more frequently by the large iron gates, scanning the faces of people passing by. She wanted to transform them into Mama or Papa or Aunt Isi.

One by one, over the weeks and months, the other girls left, always amidst a strange blend of smiles and tears. No family, Susan noted, had escaped without some tragic loss. She knew now that the rumors Julia had told them – of horrible concentration camps where people were killed by the thousands – were all true. Her unspoken fear grew. *What fate awaited her and Vera?* She hadn't told Vera what she had learned from Julia about Mama and Tomas. *Where were her parents now?*

In front of Vera, she tried to be cheerful. "Perhaps Papa and Mama have no way to get us yet," Susan tried to comfort Vera. "We just have to be patient."

Her own comfort was that Julia was still here. No one had come for her, either. It was hard to imagine that both their families had been completely destroyed. Perhaps their parents were together, getting a new home ready for them.

Julia seemed not to mind that they were still at the convent. She worked all day with a group of nuns at the arduous task of restoring their damaged walls and windows. Whatever breaks she took, she spent with Sister Klara tending to the sick who flocked to the infirmary. Susan tried to follow her example, busying herself with work.

To her own surprise, the girl Susan missed the most was Lena. Lena had been an inspiration to her – so full of both practical and creative knowledge. She was the best one at building a fire from the scraps of wood they salvaged from the wrecked walls. Lena told them great stories and showed them how to make all kinds of crafts. But most of all, Lena was a new friend, very different from the other girls she had known, and Susan appreciated this.

Soon after the German withdrawal, Lena snuck out of the convent one night. "There won't be anyone coming for me," she had said. "They have no idea where I am. Now it's time for me to find my family again."

"Do you think we'll see each other again?" Susan had asked her.

"I don't know," said Lena slowly, changing the subject. "I wonder whether I'll find my parents." Susan was surprised to hear Lena's voice thick with tears. "Do you think my little brother will still remember me?" Lena asked. "He was only three when those soldiers took them all."

"I know just how you feel," said Susan sympathetically. Though Lena had always seemed so strong and independent, Susan saw how similar Lena's feelings were to her own.

"I'm glad I came here," said Lena. "And not just because the nuns brought me back to health. It's also because I met all of you here." The next morning when they got up, Lena's bed was empty. She had gone as mysteriously as she had arrived.

That was back at the beginning of February. Now it was April and the birds were singing and green buds were bursting forth on the fruit trees. Susan looked at the dark earth, remembering Sister Agnes's words about the roots underground, already hard at work. With its chief caretaker gone, would this garden ever be the same again?

Susan never had a chance to find out.

Chapter 33

Finally

It was Julia's father, Uncle Ferenc, who finally came for them toward the end April. Susan was twelve now – almost thirteen, she liked to think.

Julia, overjoyed at seeing her father, clung to him for a long time. Susan hung back, awkwardly clutching Vera's hand. Where were her mother and father? Why had *they* not come?

Finally, Julia and her father pulled apart. They had not yet said anything to each other. Uncle Ferenc now noticed Susan and Vera standing in the background and hurried over to give them a warm embrace. He cleared his throat as if uncertain how to begin.

"Susan and Vera, I have come for you as well," he said, choosing his words carefully. "Your Mama and Papa are anxiously waiting for you at home." He hesitated, "We couldn't all come, so they asked me to bring you back. After all, we are family."

"Mama – how is Mama?" interrupted Julia, clutching his arm as if afraid he might vanish again. Uncle Ferenc ignored her question. He focused his eyes on Susan and cleared his throat again, blinking rapidly behind his glasses, fighting back tears.

"My Mama and Papa?" Susan whispered. "They are both waiting? They are both at home?" she asked incredulous. Uncle Ferenc nodded yes, without uttering a sound.

"I thought," Susan stammered, "Julia said…."

Uncle Ferenc silenced her with a light kiss on her forehead. "They will tell you what happened," he said. "Those of us who survived, we have all suffered. We must each tell our own stories now – stories of both the living and the dead." He sighed deeply. "I hope the world has the strength to hear them all."

He stepped back and spread his arms wide. "But look at you!" he smiled, his voice tinged with pride. "Look how beautiful and healthy all you girls are! Susan and Julia, you have grown into radiant young women. And Vera, you have grown so tall. You are a big girl now!"

At last, it was their turn to return to their family. But as Susan walked around saying last farewells, she found it hard to leave. She reassured Ester that surely she would hear from her boyfriend soon, tucked away a last biscuit from Sister Magda for the trip, gave Mother Gabriel a final hug. Visiting the garden for the last time, she thought about how much this place and the people in it now meant to her. Beside the deep friendships she had made, she also discovered the wonder of being part of a community that was able to work well together, despite their differences in backgrounds and religions. Even though she had been hoping to leave the convent since the day she arrived, she knew that it had changed her forever.

As they traveled back into the city, Susan was shocked at the destruction she saw. It was the first time Susan had been outside the convent grounds in a year. Crumbling, burnt out buildings, piles of bricks, and twisted metal littered every street. It seemed as if all light

Susan and Vera couldn't believe the destruction as they left the convent to go home.

The graceful Chain Bridge had been bombed.

It was rebuilt after the war.

and color had been erased off the surface of Budapest. Even Vera was speechless at the desolation.

They reached the banks of the Danube in silence. Susan found that she could not look at the river. She remembered all too clearly the young nun's words, spoken not so long ago – describing the murders she had witnessed. She didn't want to see the blood tainting the color of the Danube. She didn't want to imagine the ghosts of the men, women, and children who died here. She wanted to remember the Danube as it had been before the Nazis took over – a river full of excitement and adventure, a pathway to the rest of the world.

Since the bridges were all destroyed, they had to travel by boat to Pest. Their wait in line was long and cold. By the time there was space for them on one of the many small boats that ferried people across the city, the sun had disappeared behind the hills of Buda. As the boat drifted out from beneath the shadows of the bombed pillars of the Chain Bridge, Susan's eyes misted over. Both Mama and Papa had been so proud to live in this city.

"Budapest is the jewel of Europe," Papa used to say proudly on their Sunday morning walks. "Look at the buildings. Each one is a unique work of art, a lesson in history."

Now, Papa's jewel was reduced to a heap of rubble. She soon discovered that the ruin of the city was the least of Papa's worries.

Chapter 34

Reunion

Uncle Ferenc's steps dragged as they reached their building. To Susan's surprise, he led them right past it.

"Your family lives in a different building now," he explained. "Someone else moved into your old apartment as soon as your mother was forced to go to the ghetto. But when he came back, your father found a vacant apartment in this building, just in the next block. You are still in the same neighborhood. You will even be able to go back to your old school."

School! Susan hadn't thought about going back. She realized that Uncle Ferenc was right. She would have to start school again. Would Ildiko and those other girls who had ignored her before still be there? Would they talk to her now? How could she ever face them again?

They reached their new building. Uncle Ferenc stopped them on the steps. "Don't expect things to be the same," he said slowly, his eyes averted. "Your parents – they have gone through a lot."

His words filled Susan with foreboding. She held Vera's hand tightly as they stood in front of the door with the large brass number nailed above a frosted pane of glass. She rapped loudly on the wooden surface and held her breath.

"I will see you tomorrow," Uncle Ferenc said hurriedly, as they heard the approach of heavy footsteps from the other side. "We live just there now," he tilted his head to the right, "in the next building, Julia and I. There is much Julia and I have to talk about." Julia gave Susan a puzzled and concerned look. Then she and her father were gone.

At first, Susan did not recognize the old man who opened the door. Confused, she was about to back up and say that they had made a mistake. Perhaps they were on the wrong floor.

But then the man smiled and exclaimed, "Susan! Vera!" It was Papa's voice! Immediately they were swallowed up in his embrace. Papa's hair was snowy white. His face lined with many creases. His once-full beard was just a sparse white stubble on his chin. He was painfully thin. But it was Papa!

"Mama, can we go see Mama?" Susan and Vera asked simultaneously, once they had had their fill of hugging and looking at each other. "And where is Tomas? Can we see Tomas? Can he walk now?"

Biting his bottom lip, Papa looked at the girls and down at the floor again.

"Mama is not well," he said slowly. "And Tomas, well…" Papa seemed to be choking on his words, "Mama is not well because of Tomas. Tomas is dead." To Susan's horror, Papa began to cry in heavy, heaving sobs.

It was a terrible thing he had said. Susan and Vera were at his side again in an instant, their arms around him, and now all three of them were locked together in a tight embrace, rocking back and forth.

It was Papa who straightened up first and wiped their eyes with his handkerchief.

"We have to be strong for Mama," he said hoarsely. "She has been very depressed, barely eating or doing anything. I can't get her to leave the house. That's why I couldn't come to get you myself. I hate to leave her alone for more than just a few minutes at a time. Perhaps having you back will help her remember that there is still a future to live for. She – we both witnessed terrible things. Terrible." He shook his head sadly and his eyes had a momentary lost, frightened look. With an effort, he focused on the girls. "Go on in and see Mama. She is in the bedroom."

Vera and Susan looked at one another. Vera grabbed Susan's hand and pulled her eagerly toward the bedroom door. As they walked down the short hallway, Susan noticed how barren this apartment was. There was no sign of their old furniture, no paintings on the walls. Instead, ghostly spots loomed where a couch, shelves, and cabinets had kept the paint from yellowing. The worn hardwood floor was bare of any carpet. In the bedroom, an unmade mattress lay on the floor. Odds and ends of clothing spilled over the top of a cardboard box.

Mama sat in a chair by the window, but she was not looking outside. Her eyes stared vacantly into space. As they approached her, she made no sign of recognition. "Mama," Susan said quietly, "it's Vera and me. We've come home." Mama did not move nor did she reply.

Vera climbed into her lap and tried to snuggle against her. "Mama," she said, searching her mother's face, "Uncle Ferenc came to get us. He said I am a big girl now." Vera wiggled as she began to slip down her mother's lap to the floor.

Suddenly, Mama's arm lifted Vera to keep her from falling. With her other arm, she reached out toward Susan and pulled her close. A silent tear trickled down Mama's sunken cheek and a gentle sigh escaped her lips, as she finally embraced her girls.

Their dinner was composed of the now-familiar horse meat, some boiled potatoes, and carrots. At first, they sat in silence, heavy with the burden of the joy and sorrow of this family reunion. Papa led Mama to the table where she sat with downcast eyes, occasionally putting a small forkful of food in her mouth.

"I'm sorry, I'm not a very good cook," Papa said, watching the girls poking idly at their food.

"This is almost a feast," said Susan, "compared to the little we had to eat at the convent. I'm just not very hungry."

They remained at the table after the meal, since there was nowhere else to sit in the nearly empty apartment.

"So tell me," Papa said, breaking another lengthy silence, "tell me what it was like at the convent. What was it like for two Jewish girls living with nuns?"

"At first it was hard to be away from home," Susan explained. "But there were lots of us Jewish girls there. Very many! And the nuns, they let us light the Sabbath candles. They let us celebrate Passover." At this, both Papa and Mama looked at her in wonder.

"I am so relieved," sighed Mama. "While we were separated, it was one of my constant worries that you would come back forgetting who you were and why all this was happening."

Slowly, bit by bit, they exchanged memories of their months apart. Papa learned with increasing concern of the dangers the girls were subjected to. Susan and Vera heard about the grueling work Papa had to do at the labor camp. They told Papa about the friends they made. He shared with them the horrors of his living conditions. Susan and Vera recounted the night of the Nazi raid, their terrifying flight across the garden to the shelter, Sister Agnes's death.

Papa, his head cradled in his hands, told them of his escape from the labor camp. "We heard about the Nazi invasion of Budapest. For a long time after that, we had to work harder than ever in the mines. Each morning, I couldn't bear the thought of yet another day of back-breaking work with so little food to nourish us. It was the thought of you that kept me going." He encompassed them all with his eyes and smiled the first smile Susan had seen on his face since their return. "That gave me strength and sustained me more than the largest feast.

"Then one day we learned of the Russian advance into Eastern Europe. The Nazis began transporting people to other camps. Horrible rumors began circulating about these new camps. 'Death Camps' some people called them. They said their main purpose was to exterminate the Jewish race. The Nazis were getting desperate, fearful that their time was running out. Daily, trainloads of people were sent to the camps. Finally it was my turn. Two friends and I decided that we would never step inside one of those camps. We would rather die trying to regain our freedom than be slaughtered." Papa paused and took a deep breath. Susan could tell that it was difficult for him to relate these experiences. Though she wanted to spare him, she also wanted to know – to know everything.

"When the train stopped for supplies," her father continued, "while the guards were momentarily distracted by the promise of food and drink, we broke through a couple of rotting boards in our cattle car. We fled across the fields. There were just three of us. No one else dared follow. The guards discovered our escape almost at once. They ran after us, firing their guns. I was the fastest runner, thanks to my training with the soccer team." Papa hung his head lower and wiped his eyes.

"Both of the other men fell, shot in the back. I saw them but I couldn't stop. I ran for a long time. Bullets rained around me, but by some miracle I was not hit. I ran through the tall grass into a dense forest. Still I kept running. I have never run like that. The whole time, in my mind, I saw Mama, the two of you, and Tomas. I was running back to you."

A heavy silence fell again upon their small family sitting around the table. Susan was sure they were all thinking of the tiny life that was no longer with them. Vera moved her chair closer to Susan's, curled up, and laid her head in Susan's lap. In minutes, she was fast asleep. Tenderly, Papa picked her up and carried her to a small bedroom with a mattress on the floor, neatly made with pillows and a blanket.

Through the open doorway, Susan saw Papa lay Vera down and pull the covers up around her shoulders. She wondered how he must feel doing this ordinary act again after such a long time.

Chapter 35

Mama's Story

After Papa had put Vera to sleep, Mama began to speak. At first, Susan could barely hear her voice, it was so quiet. But it gained momentum as her story progressed.

"We were forced to move to the ghetto a few weeks after you girls left. Each of us was only allowed to pack one small suitcase. Everything else we had to leave behind: the furniture, the dishes, my paints – everything. Though it was still warm, I put on several layers of clothing so I could fill the suitcase with other things I would need. But," and here Mama gave Susan a weak smile, "before I put them on, I quickly sewed my rings and necklaces into the hems of my dresses and coat. I have managed to keep these till now. Into the suitcase, I put a couple of pots, diapers, and a bottle for Tomas.

"The conditions in the ghetto were horrible. Several families crowded together in one apartment. We had little food and little to do besides wander the streets, bartering odds and ends, and watching the growing despair in people's faces. I was more fortunate than most, since Tomas and I shared a tiny apartment with only your Aunt Margaret."

She continued her story. "Then Isi smuggled a message in, saying she would try to get food to me every few days. She said I was to walk by a certain section of the ghetto wall at dusk each day. I went there four days in a row, walking back and forth as if I was just getting some fresh air. A paper bag finally came flying over the wall on the fifth day, almost hitting me on the head. In it were bread, carrots, and a large link of sausage. After that, I went there every day at the same time and was rewarded every few days. I had hoped there would be a letter, or even a short note, giving me news of you girls or of her. But there was nothing, ever. It was too dangerous – in case someone else picked up the bag."

Without saying a word, Susan listened intently to her mother. "Meanwhile, Julia had returned. Margaret was furious with her for having left the convent, but Julia wouldn't listen to her. She stayed."

Mama continued. "Julia had a great knack for getting in and out of the ghetto unnoticed. I think she sometimes went through the sewers because she would come back stinking and filthy. She helped smuggle children out of the ghetto and into hiding. A couple of times, Julia tried to get Margaret and me to escape, but we both thought it was too dangerous.

"Then a few weeks before Margaret and I were taken away, the bags of food stopped coming. I don't know what happened to Isi. I hope she wasn't discovered." Mama's voice became quiet again, and her sentences short and clipped.

"I no longer had any bread to trade for milk for Tomas. He became ill. He was feverish and always crying. Then the Nazis rounded us up. Margaret was beside herself with fear for Julia. She made Julia hide in a cabinet."

Mama paused and took a tiny sip of water. Susan held her breath, not daring to say a word in case Mama stopped talking altogether. Papa shifted his chair closer to Mama's and put his arms around her. She glanced up at him gratefully, then continued.

"We were put on different trucks. I knew mine was headed toward death, because of Tomas and because I was so weak by then. I had caught his fever and could no longer work. I remember Margaret's last look, so full of sorrow. We both thought it would be me who died and she who still had a chance at life. Who could have known things would turn out like this?"

Susan didn't know what Mama meant with that last comment. She noticed that Mama's eyes were overflowing with tears now, but she gripped Papa's hand and, staring straight ahead, went on.

"All the people on my truck were too old or too young or too sick to be considered of value. We traveled all day without food or water. It was very hot. Tomas wasn't crying anymore. He was barely breathing. I was too ill myself to get help for him. Besides, what could anybody do?

We were all crammed into the small truck together. It was incredibly hot and airless. I was sure we would all perish before we reached our destination.

"At some checkpoint, a man in a suit came running up beside the truck as it was about to take off again. He yelled for us to stop. He said he was from the Swedish embassy. He said he had a list of people under Swedish protection. He read off the names. My name was on his list. I have no idea how my name got on that list, but there it was.

"Five of us were allowed to get off the truck and leave with him. He took us to a building where other people met us. Women were there to take care of me. They put me to bed. They fed me." Mama's voice shook as she tried to finish. "That Swedish man – Raoul Wallenberg – he saved our lives. But it was too late for Tomas. Tomas died that night."

Once again, they shared the silence and the tears. But knowing they were together again somehow helped. Susan reached for Mama's hand and kissed it.

"We should go to bed now," Papa said eventually. "We have had a long and difficult day ahead. But we are alive and we have each other. We must be thankful for that. No one has come out of this without some terrible loss."

In a softer voice, looking into Susan's eyes, he added, "Julia's mother, died in the concentration camp. In Auschwitz."

Chapter 36

Life in the City

By habit, Susan woke early, before 6:00 a.m., before anyone else. She walked silently through the barren apartment. Many things had changed. She had left her home as a frightened, resentful little girl and came back feeling confident and thankful for being alive. She was surprised to find that she didn't feel too upset by the emptiness of the apartment, by Mama's depression and Tomas's death, or by the uncertainty of their lives. Instead, she felt strangely invigorated, eager to do something to remedy their situation. Things would be difficult, she knew, but they would manage.

She turned as Papa came out from the bedroom, stretching and rubbing his eyes. Together, they looked through the cupboards and pantry at their meager supply of food.

"The first thing we have to do," Papa said gravely, "is get some groceries." They smiled at each other, glad to be partners in this endeavor. "Very few people have money right now," Papa explained. "People get what they need by trading. But, as you can see, we don't have much to trade. I got these chairs and table and mattresses," Papa waved his arm around the apartment, "by trading a couple of Mama's rings."

"Here," he reached into his pants' pocket and pulled out a shimmering string of creamy pearls. "You can trade these for some food and clothes," he said, as he handed her the pearls.

Papa picked up a loaf of bread, slicing it as he talked. Susan reached for a small pot to heat some water for their tea. "I will give you some money, as well," Papa continued, "money that I have earned by clearing away rubble and doing repairs for others."

Susan suddenly realized that Papa expected her to do all the shopping and trading while he worked. "Mama is not ready to venture outside yet," he explained. "After all that she has suffered, it has made her very sad and fearful. I will be relying on you now to shop and run errands. I know you can do this. I can tell that you have grown in many ways."

Susan flushed at the unexpected praise. She hugged Papa. "I will do my best," she promised.

Papa continued, "Also, you should know that there are medical stations where food is handed out. The line is long, but you can get a hot meal there and they will give you a container to bring some home." They finished their breakfast preparations and sat down at the table.

As they ate, Papa also told her of an abandoned store on St. Istvan Boulevard, now used to store furniture and clothing from homes that had been hastily evacuated by Jewish families when the Nazis arrived. She could go there for some warm clothing for the family.

"Just make sure we have enough food for today and tomorrow, and then trade things for whatever else you think we need. I trust you." Papa said, before he left for work.

After tidying up, making a hasty list, and saying goodbye to Mama and Vera, Susan set out. She walked the streets of her old neighborhood in a daze. It was strange to be in a busy street after the seclusion of the convent grounds. She walked by their old building and wondered who must be living there now.

She turned onto St. Istvan Boulevard and was shocked by what she saw. Several of the buildings were nothing more now than a pile of bricks, wood, and broken glass. All that remained of Margit Bridge was a couple of forlorn looking support pillars sticking out of the murky waters of the Danube. The windows of the café she and Aunt Isi had passed on their way to the convent were boarded up. Mr. Lukacs and his newsstand were gone. In their place, Russian and Hungarian soldiers now patrolled the street. For a moment, her confidence wavered. How would she know where to get the supplies she needed with everything so different?

Then, around the next corner, she saw Julia. Julia's eyes were red, and her lips were pressed in a small, straight line. For a brief moment, there was an awkward silence, and then they embraced and clung to one another other tightly. It was barely a year since they had passed each other in the city streets without exchanging a word or a smile. That was before they had shared so much at the convent. Yet, since their parting yesterday, it felt like they had both lived through another lifetime of pain.

"I'm so sorry," Susan stammered at last. "I heard about your mother, about Aunt Margaret."

"Yes, I'm sorry about your family, too," Julia said quietly. "I heard about Tomas and that your Mama is not well." They stood there for a while, first looking at the ground, then looking at each other.

"I'm getting groceries," explained Julia. "It's only my Papa and me now, and he's working…." Her voice threatened to dissolve into tears, but Susan broke in hurriedly.

Only a few pillars of Margit Bridge remained.

"Me too. I have to trade things for groceries as well. Can you help me? I've never bargained before or traded anything for food. And some of the old stores are gone." She waved her arm around at the ruin of the city.

"Sure," Julia replied, her voice under control now. "I'm an expert at getting the best deals possible. See, I traded some books we found in the apartment for a loaf of bread and these carrots." They walked off together, arm in arm.

The next few weeks were occupied with a daily struggle for survival. Each morning Susan rose early and spent a few quiet moments planning her day, checking through a list of supplies they needed. After Papa left for work, she went out in search of food, often meeting Julia on the way.

Susan was shocked to see Budapest in ruins.

Mama still refused to leave the house. "I just can't face those people," she said dejectedly. "How can I know who wanted me and my Tomas dead? I don't think I can ever look into their eyes again."

But slowly, Mama began to improve. She spent less time sitting by the window vacantly staring out into the courtyard. Gradually, she took more interest in what Susan and Vera were doing, often giving Susan specific instructions for what to buy. One day when Susan came back, there were Mama and Vera curled up on the worn couch, reading aloud from a big book of fairy tales. Another day, Susan returned to the sweet aroma of fresh poppy seed crescents just out from the oven.

On one of her daily excursions, Susan heard a strain of haunting violin music. It was coming from the small park at the northern corner of St. Istvan Boulevard and the ruined entrance to Margit Bridge. She followed the sound and joined a few bystanders who paused in front of a young Gypsy girl with a violin tucked under her chin. The music she played was a medley of both joyful and mournful melodies. To Susan, it seemed very appropriate to the mood of the war-torn city.

On the grass beside the violin player sat another girl with her head bent over a blanket displaying an assortment of handcrafted dolls. The dolls looked very familiar to Susan. The girl lifted her head and their eyes met. Lena! Immediately Lena jumped up and embraced Susan. The bystanders stared in surprise at this open display of affection between them. For the next half hour, the girls eagerly exchanged stories about the last few months.

Sadly, Susan learned that Lena's mother and father had both died in concentration camps. "This is my cousin," Lena introduced the violin player. "I live with her family now. They managed to hide out in the mountains and escape the Nazi soldiers. We are staying at a temporary camp outside the city. Every day, my aunt brings in fresh fruits and vegetables from the farmers to sell at the market. My cousin and I try to earn something extra by visiting the parks in the city." After that, Susan often met Lena and her cousin, frequently bringing them some of Mama's baked goods. In return, they gave her fresh wild berries and vegetables and, once, even a chicken from the farms.

One day, when she had relatively few chores, Susan stopped in front of their old apartment building. Swallowing her fear, she mounted the steps to the third floor. To her disappointment, the curtains were drawn over the windows that faced onto the balcony. She knocked on the door. After a few moments, heavy steps approached, and a tall woman dressed in an elegant grey suit opened the door a crack. Through that crack, Susan immediately recognized Mama's painting of the rose garden on Margit Island hanging on the wall. The sight of the picture boosted her courage.

"I used to live here before," Susan began boldly, "before the Nazi invasion. I was wondering if some of our belongings might still be here." The woman frowned down at her.

"I live here now," she said with a heavy accent. "The man at the housing office told me this apartment was vacant and I moved in. I come from Romania where life was hard. Everything here is mine. I paid for everything."

"My mother is an artist," said Susan quickly, seeing that the woman was ready to shut the door in her face. She pointed at the painting on the wall. "She painted that picture," she added with pride.

"I told you that everything here is mine now," the woman repeated as she shut the door firmly. Susan stood there, shocked at her rudeness. Slowly she turned and shuffled back along the balcony.

Just before she reached the stairwell, she heard the door creak open and the woman called out. "Girl! Come back!" She beckoned to Susan. "This I found in the bedroom closet. Here, take it." She handed Susan a large shoebox. It was filled with Mama's tubes of paint and brushes.

"Your mother, she is a good artist," said the woman more kindly. "Very good." Then she shut the door again.

That evening, Susan showed the treasures to her family. Papa promised to get some paper and maybe even a canvas for Mama.

"Our walls will look pretty again!" Vera jumped up and down delighted.

"I have some pictures that I drew at the convent," Susan said, a bit shy about her drawings. She had not mentioned the drawings that she had brought back with her. Her mother had been too wrapped up in her own sorrow. Now, Mama looked at Susan with curiosity and her face lit up, reminding Susan for a brief instant of the way Mama had looked a long time ago.

"Well, why haven't you shown them to me before?" Mama said. "Hurry up and get them."

Susan and her mother spent the next couple of hours huddled

together on the couch examining each picture, talking about the events surrounding each drawing.

"I'm so glad you drew these pictures," Mama exclaimed. "They bring your stay there to life for me. Now I don't feel so much like I've missed out on a whole year of your lives. And your drawing has really improved."

Though Susan glowed with pride at Mama's praise, it was the life in her mother's voice that meant the most to Susan.

Chapter 37

A Letter

Summer 1945

Julia and Uncle Ferenc came over frequently for dinner. After supper one evening, Uncle Ferenc announced that he and Julia would be leaving Budapest.

"I found out that Julia and I can join some others on a ship going to Palestine. Many Jews from all over Europe are going there to start a new life."

Uncle Ferenc stopped and looked intently at Mama and Papa. "Why don't you join us?"

Mama shook her head.

"I'm sorry, Ferenc, but I cannot go with you. I cannot go to a land where there might be more fighting." She hung her head. "At the same time, I can no longer live here," she said quietly. "I don't know what we are going to do." Mama buried her face in her hands.

Papa put his arms around her. Then he spoke to Ferenc "I must agree with Rose. Perhaps one day, we will come to visit…."

He and Uncle Ferenc studied each other in prolonged silence. Finally, Uncle Ferenc rose.

"Very well," he said slowly. "You and I, we have always had different dreams, my brother." Uncle Ferenc and Papa embraced. A week later he and Julia departed from Budapest.

Summer arrived with full force. The dark green foliage of the occasional tree along the sidewalk offered welcome relief from the glaring sun. Susan looked with regret toward Margit Island and the ruins of the bridge they used to cross. Her hopes of summertime picnics on the island lay shattered in the rubble. She looked across and down the river to the distant slopes of Gellert Mountain, just barely visible at the curve of the Danube. Who was tending the convent gardens now, she wondered? She picked her way slowly through the drab, dusty streets, missing Julia's company.

For a while, Susan saw Lena in the park every day. Often Susan took samples of Mama's baking for her. In return, Lena shared some of her aunt's berries and fruits. They often sat talking in the shade of the park's tall chestnut trees. But when the scorching heat of summer descended on the city, Lena and her family moved on.

One sultry August afternoon, Susan noticed a letter with unusual stamps in the mailbox when she arrived home. Who would send them a letter like that? The stamps on the one they had received from Uncle

Ferenc and Julia, announcing their safe arrival, had been very different. Yet, the handwriting on the front of this envelope had a familiar slant to it. She had seen that writing before.

She took the letter to her mother who, as soon as she saw it, grabbed it.

"That's Isi's handwriting!" she exclaimed. "She's alive!" Mama sat down on the couch and tore open the envelope. She read it aloud to Susan and Vera.

"My dearest Rose, I am writing to you from Toronto, Canada. From this great distance, it has taken me a while to find you. The news I have is old and tells me nothing of how you are. My heart aches when I think of you and Moritz and the children. I can only hope that you have all survived the horror and that this letter finds you in good health. I know you must have wondered what happened . . . why I suddenly stopped sending food over the wall. I am sorry for my hasty departure from Budapest, but some of my colleagues became suspicious about my activities. Once the Nazis occupied Budapest, people suspected of helping Jews were arrested, questioned, and killed. My situation grew too dangerous. One day I noticed that I was being followed. I was afraid of being caught and tortured for information. I was willing to risk my own life to help others, but I could not jeopardize the lives of the people I was trying to help.

Fortunately, I met someone from the Swedish Embassy, Mr. Raoul Wallenberg, who issued false passports for Jews to help them escape the country. Because of my facility with languages, he asked me if I would accompany a group of Jewish refugees on their flight to safety in Sweden. I took advantage of this opportunity. Before I left, I put your name on a list of people under Swedish Embassy protection. It was the only way I could try to help you. I hope it did. I am sorry I could not do more. From Sweden, I came to Canada, through the assistance of my brother, who had emigrated here before the Nazis took over.

Rose, I must know how you all are. I am praying that you receive this and that before long I will hear from you. Now that I am settled here and have found you, perhaps I could convince you to let me bring you all to this wonderful land. Canada is a country of great freedom and opportunity. I have a job with a social services organization that helps immigrant families resettle here. After all you have been through, it would be a fresh start. Through some people I work with, I can arrange for your family to come and join me here. I will find the funds to pay your passage and sponsor the family.

Remember, Rose, we are like family. Oh, how I long to see you and to hug the children! Your loving friend,

Isabella.

Mama, Susan, and Vera sat in stunned silence. Then Mama covered her face with her hands and burst into tears. This time Susan was not concerned. She knew they were tears of relief.

Throughout the rest of the afternoon, Mama paced the apartment, anxiously waiting for Papa's return. She flew into his arms as soon as he walked through the door, the letter in her hand. Papa read the letter standing right there in the doorway. He looked into Mama's eyes when he finished.

"Would you like to go to Canada, Rose?"

"Oh, yes!" Mama said, breathless with excitement. "We can leave all this behind," she waved her arm around the room, encompassing Budapest and all their pain of the past few years. "We could start over, forget about death, hatred, and suffering. I could walk outside again and look people in the eye."

Susan held her breath, waiting to hear what Papa would say.

"Well," Papa smiled down at Mama, "it seems to be settled, doesn't it?"

Susan hugged Vera. She would always remember her home, the convent, and the friends she made there – Julia and Anna, Ester and Lena – and Sister Agnes and all her guardian angels. But like Mama, Susan wanted to make happier memories in their life ahead. Quietly smiling to herself, Susan knew that with Aunt Isi there to help, this new adventure would be wonderful for all of them.

And she couldn't wait.

Afterword

I first heard about the convent from my mother Vera. Her story took on a new life when I saw the documentary film *Orangyalhaz* (Guardian Angel House, in Hungarian), created by the Hungarian movie producer Anna Merei. The film recounted the true events of what happened at the Convent of the Sisters of Charity of St. Vincent de Paul in the years 1944-45. In the film, several women, my mother and aunt included, recount their memories and experiences of living with the Sisters in the convent. Some of the nuns also recount their experiences of those years. What inspired me was the tale of the heroism and sacrifice of the nuns, and the atmosphere of love in which the girls lived, despite the many hardships they faced.

In 2005, I visited Budapest and the Guardian Angel House Convent to walk in the footsteps of my mother and aunt and to discover the environment where all the real events in this book unfolded. Some of the nuns who had been there during the time of the Nazi occupation of Hungary were still alive. I had the honor of meeting and speaking at length with one in particular, Sister Klari Visi. She had been a nineteen-year-old novice (student nun) at the convent during that time. With everyone else, she had lived through the air raids, the hunger, and the many other dangers of those years.

From Sister Klari I learned that after all the Jewish girls had left, the convent was forced to close, and the nuns dispersed throughout

Sister Klari and the author, Kathy Clark.

Europe. It was not until 1989 that the convent was reestablished. Only a few of the original one hundred and fifty nuns returned, Sister Klari among them. In memory of the life-saving work of the convent, she created a small museum in its basement. Several of the photographs in this book are from her museum.

While in Budapest, I also visited the site of the Jewish ghetto, the district where my mother and aunt had lived, and the school they had attended. Standing in the places where people actually experienced these stories and survived the

Exhibits in Sister Klari's museum

223

Susan and Vera

injustices of Nazism, I felt dwarfed by the heroism of the nuns, and others like them, who had risked their lives to help those in need.

More than sixty years have passed since Vera and Susan left the convent to return to their home. My mother is now a great-grand-mother. Aunt Susan is a grandmother. Both live in Toronto. But even though so many years have passed, nothing can erase their memories of those days in the convent. They remain fresh in their minds, and now I hope you will remember these examples of heroism and courage, too.

– Kathy Clark

Acknowledgments

I could not have written this book without the help and support of many people.

I want to thank:

Anna Merei, the producer of the documentary movie *Orangyalhaz* or 'Guardian Angel House' for letting me retell the events so dramatically recorded in her film.

My mother and aunt, who answered my endless stream of questions and gave me a true sense of what living in the convent during the Holocaust felt like. I also appreciate their permission to use their photos in this book.

The City of Ottawa Arts Council, whose financial grant made it possible for me to travel to Hungary and explore the real Guardian Angel House.

The Sisters of Charity of St. Vincent de Paul in Budapest, for their hospitality and their willingness to supply me with information; especially Sister Klari Visi who, for me, embodied the vitality and dedication of the Sisters of Charity to serve those in need.

My close friend and editor, Paddy Dupuis, who helped me with the original manuscript and who patiently guided me through many revisions.

My first three young readers, Sarah DeKorte, Anna Gareis and Anna Dupuis, who gave me feedback on the age appropriateness of the first draft.

Sarah Swartz, my editor at Second Story Press who repeatedly helped to clarify and simplify my work.

Margie Wolfe and the staff at Second Story Press, for their enthusiastic support and their dedication in bringing the book to completion.

And finally, my family for their constant encouragement and the many sacrifices they made, giving me the time and space I needed to do the writing. They have some loving ownership in these pages.